INCHTINN

I SLAND OF
SHADOWS

Danny Weston

INCHTINN

ISLAND OF SHADOWS

Illustrated by MIRANDA HARRIS

uclanpublishing

Inchtinn: Island of Shadows is a uclanpublishing book

First published in Great Britain in 2019 by
uclanpublishing
University of Central Lancashire
Preston, PR1 2HE, UK

978-1-9129790-5-9

1 3 5 7 9 10 8 6 4 2

Set in 10/17pt Kingfisher by Becky Chilcott

A CIP catalogue record for this book is available from the British Library.

Printed and bound in Great Britain by Clays Ltd, Elcograf S.p.A.

For Philip Caveney,
without whom I would never have
become a writer . . .

"You cannot swim for new horizons until you have courage to lose sight of the shore."

William Faulkner

Chapter One

The Boat

NOAH STOOD ON THE WOODEN JETTY IN THE chill light of early morning. He stared apprehensively across the vast stretch of flat grey water to the distant smudge on the horizon that Mr Morrison had just pointed out as their eventual destination. Noah pulled the canvas lifejacket tighter around him and tried not to tremble. He didn't want the old man to know how scared he was, but realised that it was probably all too obvious. It clung to him like a bad smell, like an ill-fitting suit of clothes that he could never remove, no matter how hard he tried.

Mr Morrison sat in the wooden dinghy, smiling encouragingly up at Noah. The boat was already piled high with all the equipment that Millicent had insisted on bringing with them and she was still in the house, selecting a last few items that she couldn't bear to be parted from, even for a couple of weeks. Noah couldn't believe she was planning on bringing out yet more things. Didn't she realise how dangerous it was to overload a boat? Didn't she know how deep the Firth of Forth actually was?

"Not a good sailor then?" observed Mr Morrison, in his slow Scottish lilt. "Despite the name," he added under his breath, and Noah winced, already too familiar with the joke or at least, variations on it. He had heard them so many times back at his last boarding school. "Noah who's afraid of the water," they used to whisper, just loud enough for him to hear. It was one of his main reasons for leaving the place.

"Weather's good, anyway," added Mr Morrison. "Should be a nice calm crossing. That's always a blessing." He leaned over the side of the boat and spat into the water. He was old and grey-whiskered, his scrawny body encased in a voluminous, khaki duffel coat. A woolly hat was pulled down to just above his piercing blue eyes. He claimed to be an experienced sailor – that's what he'd told Millicent, anyway – but Noah was far from convinced. People in the local village, he thought, would claim just about anything if they thought it was an easy way of earning a few extra pounds; but whatever Mr Morrison had told Millicent about his abilities on the water, she'd booked him for the trip and paid up front in hard cash. Now here he sat in a boat that looked decrepit enough to fall to pieces at any moment.

He studied the floating speck of phlegm he'd just expelled as though trying to spot a hidden message in it. Then he turned back to study Noah, who thought he detected a hint of malice in the old man's gaze as he said, "Well, you may as well climb aboard now. If you're ready."

And suddenly Noah was back at the school, standing on the high diving board and staring down at the blue water of the swimming pool below him, while Mr Greer, the PT instructor glared up at him, no doubt wondering what was taking so long. Noah's grinning classmates clustered around Mr Greer, enjoying the moment.

"Well, come on, boy, what are you waiting for? It's quite simple. Put your blessed head down and dive!" Greer's voice echoed around the swimming pool and Noah was horribly aware of the other boys sniggering at his discomfort, knowing only too well about his fear of the water.

He couldn't move so much as a muscle. He stood like a statue, rooted in position, absolutely terrified of the prospect of diving from the board. He didn't exactly know what he was afraid of. There was just something about the prospect of the chill embrace of the water that filled him with a powerful sense of dread – the thought that he would slide into those glistening depths and never ever manage to find his way back to the surface.

"Are ye alright, lad?" Mr Morrison's concerned voice brought Noah back to the present. He was relieved to find that he was standing on the jetty and not the diving board – and yet, even the thought of climbing down that short stretch of ladder into the dinghy was enough to strike an all-consuming fear into him. He opened his mouth to speak but nothing emerged.

"Do ye want me to come up there and help ye down?" asked Mr Morrison gently; and Noah realised that there was no spite in the old man at all, that he really was only trying to help.

Noah shook his head. "I'm . . . fine," he croaked. "Just . . . give me a minute. I don't . . . it's just that I don't like to be rushed."

He managed to take a tentative step forward and place one foot on the top rung of the ladder. Then gathering his courage, he swung himself around, so that he was facing back towards the jetty. He clutched the wooden uprights of the ladder so tightly they hurt his palms.

"So it's all to do with another book, is it?" asked Mr Morrison. "I believe that's what Mrs Palmer told me. Another of her stories for wee children." Noah realised that the old man was just making conversation, trying to take Noah's mind off the situation. "I'm told that she's quite a big name in publishing."

Noah nearly laughed at that innocent remark. One of the reasons why Millicent had taken to spending so much time in her remote Scottish cottage was for the novelty of not being recognised. Back home in Kent, she could barely go out of the house without being spotted by crowds of avid readers who wanted nothing more than to talk to the creator of *The Adventurers* and countless other bestselling children's series. And now a new Adventurers title was required and Millicent was planning to do something based around the exploration of a mysterious island – but, instead of just making things up like she used to, now she had decided she actually needed to spend time in just such a place. And luckily, there was one only a few miles from the cottage. The visit to Inchtinn had been planned for quite a while. Millicent had intended to visit the place alone, but Noah's unexpected arrival from the boarding school in England meant that she was now obliged to take her adopted son along with her for the trip. It was evident she wasn't keen on the idea but she'd dealt with it in her usual brisk style, clearly determined to make the best of things.

"You can be my assistant," she'd told Noah. "You can do the fetching and carrying while I get on with the important job of writing the book."

"But I'll be bored!"

"Nonsense. The fresh air will do you good – and it'll give you a chance to ponder your latest misadventure."

It was all settled; and it had only recently occurred to Noah that there was only one way of visiting an island. You went by boat.

"I can't imagine what made her choose Inchtinn," continued Mr Morrison, watching intently as Noah slowly descended the ladder. "I mean, she said she wanted somewhere remote but that place has such a reputation . . ."

Noah froze in the act of lowering his foot to the next rung of the ladder. He actually managed to turn his head to look down into the boat.

"R . . . reputation?" he echoed. "What does that mean?"

Mr Morrison must have seen the anxiety written large in the boy's eyes and he made a dismissive gesture. "Ah . . . superstitious nonsense," he said. "Nothing for you to worry about. People like their spooky stories, that's all." He gazed up at Noah. "You're doing fine," he said. "That's the way, no hurry. Take it one step at a time."

Noah felt annoyed that his fear was so evident, but was determined not to embarrass himself. "Tell me," he insisted, as he got his left foot into position. "What they . . . say about the island."

Mr Morrison seemed reluctant to go into more detail. "Oh, you know . . . just . . . the usual claptrap," he said. "People with too much time on their hands will always take the opportunity to gossip. I'm afraid that's the way of things out here." He made another attempt to dismiss the subject. "A couple more rungs now and you're there."

Noah held his breath. He turned his head briefly to get his bearings, then lowered one foot gingerly down the last few inches onto the deck of the boat. Immediately, he felt the wood sway treacherously under his step and he teetered on the verge of panic, but Mr Morrison, sensing his fear, got quickly to his feet and stretched out a hand to support the boy, then helped to lower him onto a seat in the stern. Noah sat there miserably, his hands clamped onto the wooden thwart, aware of the way the bottom boards tipped and lurched beneath the soles of his shoes and knowing only too well that it would be much worse once they were under way.

"Are ye not much of a swimmer then?" asked Mr Morrison; and once again, Noah was back at the school, Mr Greer's harsh words booming in his ears, ordering him to dive – and then the teacher's echoing tones were joined by the rising chant of the other boys, as they clapped their hands in an urgent rhythm and urged him on. "Dive, Noah, dive, dive, DIVE!" And he'd been so desperate not to disgrace himself that he'd actually tried to go through with it. He'd snatched in a breath and allowed himself to fall. There'd been a brief horrible tumble through the air, the shocking embrace of the icy water as it struck him like a clenched fist, his breath exploding out from him with the impact – and then he'd sunk like a stone to the bottom of the pool. Worst of all, was the shock of the moment when he'd instinctively tried to suck in a breath and foul-tasting water had gushed into his mouth . . . in that instant, he'd truly believed he was going to drown.

"Are you cold?" asked Mr Morrison. "You're shaking."

"I'm all right," Noah assured the old man, but he wasn't, because in his head he was still back there, thrashing and kicking helplessly in the water, unable to claw his way back to the surface and he was terrified, more scared than he'd ever been in his fourteen years of existence. It was only then that Mr Greer had realised Noah's predicament and had dutifully dived in to pull him out. The other lads had helped to get him up out of the pool and he'd lain on his back, coughing up chlorinated water, while his classmates stood around, gazing down at him, making no attempt to hide their expressions of pure contempt. And Noah had realised at that moment that this was the way the other boys would always see him now, that there was no use trying to fit in with them anymore. He would be forever marked as a coward, and therefore not worthy of their friendship.

He'd left the school the very next day.

A gull shrieked in the air high above him, wrenching him back to the present. He stared into the sky for a moment, then lowered his gaze to look at Mr Morrison, meaning to ask once again about the island – about what he had meant by the word "reputation" – but the old man was looking back across the expanse of the jetty as somebody came down the steps of the cottage and walked confidently towards the water's edge.

"Here's your mother now," said Mr Morrison.

Chapter Two

Millicent

SHE STRODE ALONG THE NARROW STRETCH OF the jetty, carrying a large suitcase with one hand and the handle of her trusty Underwood typewriter in the other. As ever, she was dressed in a tweed jacket and jodhpurs, a slouch hat pulled down low over the grey eyes that always bore that characteristic look of steely determination. She was Millicent Palmer and she was a publishing legend, an author for more than thirty years now.

Of course, some things had changed over those years. Once upon a time, she had been ridiculously successful. Where most authors thought they were doing well to produce ten books, her titles had numbered in the hundreds and commanded the kind of sales that made the competition envious. Where other writers struggled to complete a few pages of text, she had seemed to exhale them, turning out some of her most successful stories in a matter of days. When she had a book 'on the go', as she liked to call it, she would lock herself in her study and type like someone possessed until she could key the words THE END at the foot of the final page. The books had earned her a fortune and had bought Millicent and her late husband, Archie, a splendid house in Kent, an apartment in London and a country retreat in Scotland, where they would head whenever they had a little time on their hands and needed some solitude.

Millicent and Archie had enjoyed a long and faithful marriage – and they'd been successful at everything they'd attempted with one notable exception. They had somehow failed to produce any children.

Noah had been adopted as a baby. He'd known about it from an early age, it had never been kept a secret from him. Indeed, Millicent (he never called her anything else, she hated "Mother") had once told him that she and "The Captain" – her pet name for Archie – had always intended to adopt more children, but once they'd got Noah, they'd quickly decided that one was quite enough, thank you. Noah was never really sure whether to take this as an insult or a compliment but hoped it was the latter.

And then of course, Archie had been killed in the war and that had affected Millicent profoundly. She no longer found it quite such a breeze to write her books – now it was a chore, something she really had to apply herself to. The words that had once come so easily had to be dragged out of her, one at a time. At first she had thought it would be a temporary thing, but Archie had been gone seven years now and still she was struggling to meet her deadlines. Her literary agent, Alicia, had even discussed with her the possibility of employing ghost writers who would produce new books using her name, but Millicent had resisted such a solution, assuring Alicia that she would eventually recapture her old spirit.

At the heart of it, of course, was the fact that Millicent was lonely. She had always told her friends that Archie had been the only man for her and she really wasn't interested in finding a replacement. The problem was, she wasn't particularly good at the motherhood side of things. Noah had always got on much better with Archie, who he remembered as a big, affable bearded man with a booming laugh and a joke for every occasion. Of course, there had been that unfortunate business with the sailing trips, but . . . he'd surely meant well enough with that, following some wartime notion of turning his boy into a man, and all in all, he'd been a good father, kind and supportive.

When the destroyer he'd commanded had been sunk by a torpedo in 1944, and lost with all hands, it had left a gaping hole in the family unit that would probably never be filled.

After that, Millicent had tried to fulfil her motherly duties to the best of her abilities. But things had been strained to say the very least and as soon as Noah was old enough, she'd packed him off to the first of what was to be a whole series of boarding schools. The problem was, he couldn't seem to get along at any of them. The last one had been a particularly horrible example of the form, rife with bullying and excessive corporal punishment, so he was glad to have left it behind him. But the prospect of being trapped on an island with Millicent for two weeks wasn't exactly his idea of a good time, either. He'd even suggested to her that he might stay at the cottage by himself, or that Millicent might hire somebody to look in on him every day. But she was having none of that. She wanted Noah where she could keep an eye on him.

She reached the ladder and gazed down into the ramshackle dinghy, as though assessing its suitability for the task at hand. Much to Noah's bewilderment, she seemed perfectly happy with what she was looking at. She set aside her typewriter and handed the suitcase down to Mr Morrison, who stood upright to reach for it. He grunted as he took the weight in his arms.

"Heavy," he observed, unnecessarily. He turned and

placed the suitcase carefully in the boat beside a pile of other equipment.

"Do we really need that?" asked Noah, anxiously. "It'll sink the boat."

"Nonsense," said Millicent. "It's just warm clothes and other necessities. This good weather might not hold. One needs to be prepared for all eventualities." She picked up her precious typewriter, turned around and came effortlessly down the ladder as though it was something she did all the time. She actually jumped the last couple of feet and the impact of her boots on the bottom boards made the dinghy rock alarmingly.

"Be careful, you'll capsize us!" protested Noah. Millicent and Mr Morrison exchanged amused looks.

"As you'll have gathered," said Millicent, "Noah is not a natural sailor."

"Ah, he'll be fine," said Mr Morrison. "He'll soon get his sea legs." He winked at Noah, but when he failed to get a reaction, he took a last look around. "Well, if you're all set, we might as well be on our way."

"Excellent." Millicent settled herself down beside Noah and watched as Mr Morrison moved to the stern of the boat and stooped to pull the cord of the rusty outboard motor. It took him several attempts, but finally the thing sputtered into noisy, noxious life puffing out a cloud of oily smoke. Mr Morrison cast off the mooring rope and settled himself on the stern thwart so he could handle the rudder. He opened the throttle and the dinghy moved smoothly forward across the mirror-like surface. Noah felt a corresponding lurch in his stomach and tried to put his mind on something else.

"Noah, you've gone decidedly pale," observed Millicent. "Did you take the tablets I gave you?"

Noah nodded, but didn't reply for the moment. He glanced over his shoulder and was shocked to see that the jetty was already surprisingly distant.

The tablets were supposed to help with travel sickness, but he didn't know if they were having any effect on him.

"Just keep your gaze fixed on the horizon," Millicent advised him. "I always remember Archie saying that helped."

"That would be your late husband, would it?" asked Mr Morrison, spotting an opportunity for conversation. "Somebody told me he was in the service."

Millicent nodded. "A naval officer," she said. "A Scotsman like yourself. Captain Archie McCallum." She smiled proudly. "He gave his life in defence of his country and died a hero at the Battle of the Atlantic."

Mr Morrison bowed his head. "Oh, I'm sorry for your loss," he said. Then a puzzled expression crossed his face. "Forgive me, but . . . I understood your name was Palmer?"

Millicent nodded. "It's really quite simple. I never took my husband's name. I had already established a career with my maiden name, you understand, so we decided not to er . . ." She smiled. ". . . rock the boat."

"I see," said Mr Morrison. "And you're allowed to do that, are you?"

"It's not unheard of," Millicent assured him.

"Well, well. I never knew."

"Ah, anyway, it's all ancient history now," said Millicent. "We have to get on with things. But we do miss him terribly, don't we Noah?" She glanced at her adopted son, but his head was bowed, and he was staring intently at his feet, so she made an effort to shrug off her sad memories, and turned her gaze back to Mr Morrison "So," she said. "Tell me more about this place we're visiting."

Mr Morrison frowned as though this was a tall order. "Inchtinn?" he murmured. "Well, where would I start? It's always been there on the horizon, just about as long as I can remember. Why, when I was a wee boy, I'd sail over to it with my father, looking for bird's eggs."

"You collected them?" asked Millicent.

Mr Morrison snorted. "We ate them," he said. "Times were hard back then, you were glad of anything you could get your hands on. Strange, lonely old spot, it is. Something quite eerie about it."

Millicent looked thrilled. "Good. That's exactly what I'm looking for. And the place we'll be staying?"

"It's an old wooden cabin," said Mr Morrison. "Don't be expecting too much, now. There's a cast iron stove in it and a couple of old beds and that's about it."

"I'm sure we'll be fine there," said Millicent. "And I seem to remember you said that the island is completely uninhabited?"

"Mmm . . . aye, pretty much."

Millicent looked at the old man suspiciously. "What's that supposed to mean?" he asked him. "Either it is or it isn't."

"Well, there's just the one fellow who spends some of his time out there. Finlay, his name is. The bird-man."

"The what?" Millicent looked amused.

"Oh, you know, he's a . . . what's the word? Orni . . . thol . . . ogist? I think that's what he calls himself. There are rare birds on the island, you see. He works for the Royal Society. You know, the people who look after our feathered friends? They'd take a very dim view of my old egg-stealing ways, I'm sure."

"Quite right too," said Millicent. "That's how a species becomes rare in the first place."

"Anyhow, I doubt he'll bother you at all. Stays on the far side of the island, he does, well away from the cabin you'll be using. He's got a wee shed there would make your place look like the Grand Hotel by comparison."

Millicent nodded. "He sounds interesting," she said. "Maybe I'll look him up for a chat. Might give me some useful background for the book."

"Aye, well, I wouldn't bother if I were you," said Mr Morrison. "He's a bit of a loner to tell you the truth. Well, you'd need to be, living out there most of the year. He comes back over to the mainland from time to time. I think he has a sister in Fife. He had me ferry him over once." Mr Morrison grimaced. "Not much of a conversationalist, that one."

"I suppose he doesn't get much practice," said Millicent. She smiled. "And that's it as far as habitation goes?"

"Aye. There are some abandoned buildings, mind you, up on the cliffs. Part of the old leper hospital . . ."

That made Noah sit up and take notice. "A leper hospital?" he repeated, incredulously. "In Scotland?"

Mr Morrison grinned. "Aye, it does sound odd in this day and age, I'll grant you," he admitted. "But this would have been back in the . . . what, 1500? They used to send the lepers and plague victims over from the mainland, to try and prevent the spread of the disease. You know, quarantine." He shook his head. "Grim times," he muttered.

"Oh, that's lovely," said Noah. He shot an accusing look at Millicent. "What kind of a place are you taking us to?" he asked her.

Millicent laughed at his horrified expression. "Don't worry, dear, it was all a very long time ago. I'm sure there's nothing for you to worry about." She turned her attention back to Mr Finlay. "Was Inchtinn fortified during the war?" she asked.

"I believe some of the islands were."

"Aye, some of the bigger ones. Inchcolm still has gun emplacements on it. Inchmickery, too. They were put there in case the Germans ever decided to attack Scotland but it never came to that, thank goodness."

"Why are they all called Inch-something?" muttered Noah. "Is it because they're small?"

"It just means "island", dear," said Millicent. "In Gaelic."

"Well, *Innis* would be more correct," said Mr Morrison. He smiled slyly. "Inch is what's called an Anglicisation. A lot of that sort of thing going on these days, I'm afraid." He must have sensed that she might be offended and added, "Not that I've got any problem with it. There's room for all comers here." He seemed to remember something. "We always used to call the place Shadow Island when we were youngsters."

"Why did you call it that?" asked Millicent, intrigued.

"Oh, it was just something about the way the light was when it shone on the crags. It made these extraordinary long shadows. Sometimes, you'd swear they looked like fantastic creatures . . . fairies, unicorns . . . you name it."

"So is that what Inchtinn actually means?" asked Millicent.

"Ah no. It's actually named after the lepers."

"What do you mean?" asked Noah.

"It means, literally . . . 'Island of the Sick'."

"Oh great," murmured Noah.

But there's nothing like that going on over there these days, surely?" reasoned Millicent.

"Oh, Lord no. That all happened centuries ago. Now it's just a home for sea birds and . . ."

" . . . crackpot children's authors," offered Millicent and the two of them laughed conspiratorially.

"What I don't understand," muttered Noah, looking accusingly at Millicent, "is why you feel you need to *go* there. You used to be able to write anywhere."

Millicent sighed. "I do hope you're not going to complain for the entire two weeks," she said. "It's as I've already explained. The publishers have set a ridiculous deadline for the new Adventurers book and there's just too many distractions, even at the cottage. Alicia seems to phone me every ten minutes about some nonsense or other – readers wanting signed photographs, businesses asking if I'll endorse their products and goodness knows what else. I get deluged with fan mail on a daily basis. I swear people must think my books write themselves!"

The dinghy hit a sudden swell and bucked alarmingly in the water. Noah clung on tightly, wishing this part could be over – but though he could already see the island more clearly, it didn't appear to be very much closer. "How long does it take?" he murmured. "To get there?"

Mr Morrison shrugged. "Thirty minutes . . . maybe forty. Depends on the prevailing winds."

Noah scowled. He was finding the old man's vagueness annoying.

"And how far is it?"

"Just over a mile."

"Well, how long before . . .?" Noah broke off. Mr Morrison was gazing intently down over the side of the dinghy, a big smile on his face. "Looks like we have a visitor," he said.

Noah turned his head and couldn't help giving a gasp of surprise. A dark, whiskery face was staring up at him from the water, two round black eyes watching him with intense curiosity. Noah supposed he shouldn't really be surprised. He'd seen grey seals often enough from the beach, but he'd never been this close to one before. Impulsively, he lifted one hand from the thwart to point at the creature; and the seal, no doubt interpreting this as a hostile action, flipped over and dived into the deep, its speckled carcass briefly visible below the surface like a fleeting ghost.

"You scared her off!" exclaimed Mr Morrison delightedly.

"*Her*?" repeated Millicent. "How can you tell it's a she?"

Mr Morrison waggled his thick eyebrows. "By the shape of her," he said, but he didn't elaborate on that point. "Who knows? Maybe she's a selkie, looking to visit somebody on shore."

Noah frowned, fascinated despite himself. "What's a selkie?" he asked.

The old man chuckled. "Oh, just one of those daft old

Scottish myths," he said. "Have you not heard the tale?"

Noah and Millicent both shook their heads. "Why don't you tell us?" suggested Millicent.

"Oh, I'd hesitate to recite something in front of a professional author," said Mr Morrison. "I'm afraid my storytelling skills are somewhat lacking in polish." But it was clear that he really wanted to tell them – and after a moment's hesitation, he did, leaning forward in his seat as though to confide a secret.

"The story goes that the selkies are only seals as long as they are in the water. But when they go on to the land, something incredible happens. Something mysterious. They shed their skins and turn into beautiful young women. They go further ashore, seeking the handsome young men of the area. They have romances with them. Sometimes they marry, even have children. And things carry on like that for many years. But one day, the call of the sea is too strong for the selkie. She cannot help herself. She creeps out of her home one starless night and the poor husband, out looking for his wife, finds nothing but her clothes, left carelessly on the shore – and he knows that the selkie could resist the call of the wild no longer. She has gone back to her home in the deep."

There was a short silence then as Noah and Millicent let the words sink in.

"Mr Morrison," said Millicent, after a few moments. "I do believe we'll make an author of you yet."

Chapter Three

The Island

AFTER WHAT SEEMED TO NOAH LIKE HOURS OF tense, white-knuckle sailing they finally began to draw near to Inchtinn and he was able to make out the island in more detail. It jutted up from the foaming water like a decayed tooth. Away to the right-hand side of it (or what Mr Morrison kept referring to as "starboard"), the land inclined steeply upwards to a stretch of jagged grey cliffs. Mr Morrison told Noah that they were made of something called basalt.

Straight ahead of the boat, Noah could see a gently sloping stretch of shingle beach and off to one side of it, a small inlet with a mouldering wooden jetty. Some distance back from that, was a building. Noah could make out a low wooden affair with an olive-coloured roof, covered with patches of what looked like multi-coloured moss. A single stone chimney jutted up from the centre of it. The place somehow managed to look grim and foreboding even in the bright morning sunlight.

"That's where you'll be staying," announced Mr Morrison, cheerfully. He caught Noah's apprehensive look and added: "I know it doesn't look much from here but as far as I'm aware, the roof is sound and there's a cast iron stove, if it should get cold at night. I'll make sure you have plenty of firewood before I leave." He swung the rudder to one side and the boat turned sharply to starboard.

"Aren't we going to the jetty?" asked Millicent, puzzled.

"We are, but we need to head in along the west side of the island," explained Mr Morrison. "Under the cliffs. The water's much deeper there." He pointed to a spot some ten feet or so in front of the shingle beach. "There's a line of sharp rocks just under the surface," he said and, sure enough, Noah thought he could discern areas of dark grey beneath the waterline. "They'd easily rip the bottom out of this old tub," he added. "And then we'd be in a fine old mess." He fixed Noah with a sharp look. "You remember that," he said. "Not everybody knows about it. We had some tourists a few years back in a fancy yacht, thought they'd have themselves a wee picnic on

Inchtinn. Tried to sail straight up to that jetty." He shook his head. "Big mistake."

"What happened to them?" asked Noah anxiously.

Mr Morrison frowned. "Let's just say that they came to a sticky end," he said. "And their fine yacht was good for nothing but firewood."

"So it's not really safe to go into the water?" observed Millicent, sounding disappointed. "That's a pity."

"Oh, if you fancy a swim at any time, there's an easy path down from the cliff to a wee cove," said Mr Morrison. "I'll point out the place as we head in."

"I won't be doing any swimming," Noah assured him.

"But I might," said Millicent. "I've packed our costumes, anyway. I find an early morning dip very bracing . . . and very good for the old creative juices." Noah felt like slapping her. Did she always have to be so fearless about everything?

"Well, they say the salt water is very good for the skin," said Mr Morrison. "My poor departed mother always swore by it and she lived well into her nineties."

"And is there no Mrs Morrison at home?" asked Millicent slyly.

The old man shook his head. "Never found the right woman," he said, matter-of-factly. "Oh, which is not to say I didn't spend plenty of time . . . and plenty of money, looking." He chuckled and swung the rudder back again. The boat turned sharply to port. They were right under the shadow of the cliffs now and the sun seemed to be momentarily extinguished. Noah felt a chill settle around his shoulders like a disagreeable blanket. He tilted back his head and stared upwards, noticing that there were openings in the rocks up there, dark fissures that pocked the grey stone like some kind of infection. He was about to comment on them, when his eye caught movement and just for a moment, he thought he saw somebody standing in one of the larger openings and looking down at them. He caught a brief glimpse of a grey-cloaked figure, a large hood obscuring the face of whoever it was – but then the watcher ducked back into the shadow of the cave mouth and was gone.

Noah felt strangely unsettled. Who was it, he wondered? The bird-watching fellow that Mr Morrison had mentioned? What was his name? Finlay? It could only be him, since the island was supposed to be otherwise uninhabited. But why would he act in such a secretive way? Noah opened his mouth to mention what he had seen but Mr Morrison spoke first.

"There, you see? Lovely wee spot, a regular suntrap." He was pointing to a small rocky cove, where there was indeed a beach made of what looked like fine white sand.

"How lovely!" exclaimed Millicent. "Who'd have suspected it was there? And how would a person get to it, I wonder?"

"It's easy enough to find," Mr Morrison assured her. "There's a wee garden at the back of the shack and you'll see a path leading off to the right and heading uphill. Just follow it to the cliff top and you'll soon find a track zig-zagging all the way down to the beach."

"How do you know so much about this place?" asked Noah – and his suspicion must have been evident because Millicent gave him a reprimanding look.

"Mind your manners," she told him.

"Oh, it's no bother," Mr Morrison assured her. "Really." He smiled at Noah. "I used to come to this place a lot when I was around your age. Me and my best pals would borrow my dad's old boat and we'd spend the summer days here, swimming from that very beach. At night we'd light a campfire and we'd sit around it, telling each other spooky stories."

"And did you ever stay in the cabin?" asked Millicent.

"Oh, not then! The place was a complete ruin, no roof on it. It was only years later that it was fixed up for habitation." He laughed, as though remembering. "No, we preferred to sleep out on the sand. I had some good friends, back then. All gone now, of course."

"Gone where?" asked Noah, misunderstanding. Then Mr Morrison's serious look explained everything.

"Oh, I'm, sorry," said Noah, aware of his face reddening. "I . . . I wasn't thinking."

"Ach, that's all right," Mr Morrison assured him. "You're just a slip of a lad. Why would you be pondering on such gloomy matters? But, I'm afraid, when you get to my age it becomes a daily preoccupation. Whose turn is it next?" He sighed, shook his head, then seemed to realise how gloomy he sounded and made an effort to lighten the tone. "So, here's the jetty," he announced, a little too loudly. "Let's get you unpacked, shall we?"

He nosed the dinghy in alongside the wooden platform and tethered it upright. He moved to the side of the boat and helped Millicent and then Noah to clamber out onto the wooden deck. Noah let out a long sigh of relief at the feel of the solid boards beneath his feet. He turned back to the boat and Mr Morrison began to hand up the various items of luggage to him.

"We'll have to make a few trips, I'm afraid," said Millicent. She looked at Noah. "You can take off the lifejacket now, I'm sure Mr Morrison will want to keep that on the boat with him."

Noah dutifully unlaced the canvas lifejacket and handed it down to Mr Morrison, who stowed it in the stern of the dinghy. Millicent shrugged a rucksack onto her shoulders and then lifted the biggest suitcase. She instructed Noah to pick up a cardboard box full of provisions and watched as Mr Morrison climbed out of the boat, displaying remarkable agility for a man of his age. He picked up a large mahogany box and looked at it curiously.

"It's a wind-up gramophone," explained Millicent. "I like to have a bit of music when I write. Helps with the old inspiration."

"What kind of music?" asked Mr Morrison, leading the way along the jetty.

"Classical. You can't beat a bit of Bach, don't you think?"

Mr Morrison looked blank. "I'm fond of drum and pipe bands myself."

"Is that a fact?" There was a diplomatic silence, broken only by the sounds of their feet crunching on the shingle as they walked the short distance up the beach and approached the wooden shack. Close up, it looked even more dilapidated. There were a couple of grimy windows and the cast iron guttering that edged the low roof was broken in places. Mr Morrison set down the gramophone on top of an old rain barrel and reached up to a spot between the guttering and the roof. He felt around for a moment and when he withdrew his hand, he was clutching a rusty old key. "Still here," he said. He slotted the key into the front door and with a slight effort, managed to turn the lock.

"Who actually owns the place now?" asked Millicent. "I did ask you before, but I don't recall the answer."

Mr Morrison shrugged his shoulders. "I don't rightly know," he said. "There *was* an old fellow lived out here before the war, but he died and as far I'm aware, he had no family. After that, people used it whenever they came across here. You know, walkers, bird-fanciers and the like. But not many people do that anymore, especially since Finlay and his bunch started getting overprotective of the birds. These days, I suppose it's open to whoever knows about it and chooses to stay here. People like yourselves." He pushed the door open. "We'll take a wee look inside, shall we?"

He picked up the gramophone and led the way. Millicent followed but Noah paused for a moment, to take a last look around. For some inexplicable reason, he had the distinct impression that somebody was watching him. But gazing from left to right, he could see only the shingle beach ahead of him and the dinghy, rocking gently on the grey water beside the jetty. Away to his left, the dark cliffs reared up in a jagged line against clear blue sky. From inside, he heard Millicent exclaim, "Oh, it's absolutely perfect!" There was a pause and then she spoke again. "Noah, what are you doing out there? Come and have a look!"

He sighed, shook his head. He had the strangest feeling about this place. It seemed to him that something bad was going to happen here. But he knew it would be pointless to say anything to Millicent. She would just think he was being his usual faint-hearted self. He supposed there was nothing he could do but go along with things and hope for the best.

Gathering his courage, he went inside.

Chapter Four

The Cabin

NOAH STOOD THERE, LOOKING SLOWLY AROUND. Part of him was hoping that Millicent would announce that she'd changed her mind; that they would turn around, climb in the boat and head straight back to the mainland. Except that was clearly never going to happen, because Millicent was pacing around the gloomy interior of the cabin like a child who had just woken up on Christmas morning to find that Santa had left everything she'd ever wanted.

"Look at this place, Noah!" she cried. "It's exactly what I'd pictured."

"I'm looking," he assured her flatly. What he could see was a single, low-roofed room, furnished only by a dusty pine table and four rickety wooden chairs. Daylight came in through the grimy glass of a single window beside the entrance door. To his right, there was a stone hearth into which was set a rusty cast iron stove. An open bucket half-filled with logs stood beside it. Directly ahead of them a doorway led into a second room. The door was half-open and Noah could see the foot of a single bedstead covered by a grubby mattress. Mr Morrison pointed to a doorway at the other end of the room. "There's a wee box room through there," he said, "with another bed in it. The window looks out onto the back garden." There was a disagreeable smell in the place, an odour of damp and decay, but Millicent didn't seem in the least bit put off by it. She had set her suitcase and typewriter down beside the table and was unslinging the rucksack from her back.

"Here's the table where the Adventurers will eat their meals," she announced dramatically, referring to her fictional characters, as she so often did, as if they were real people. "Douglas will, of course, be the one to keep that stove supplied with fuel! Sally will be in her element, cooking, cleaning, making the place homely . . ."

Noah shook his head. "It's a shame we haven't got her here with us now," he said scathingly.

"It *is* a little dusty," admitted Millicent. "But I brought plenty of cleaning products. We'll open some windows to air the place, slap a bit of Dettol around and we'll soon have it looking spick and span." She glanced quizzically at Mr Morrison. "What do we do about cooking?" she asked him.

Mr Morrison set the gramophone down on the table and indicated a couple of greasy looking pans hanging above the fireplace. "You heat your food on the wood stove," he said. "It's a bit primitive, I'm afraid. You won't be making any fancy meals on that."

"There isn't even a *sink*," observed Noah incredulously.

Mr Morrison nodded. "No, but there's a pump out in the backyard," he explained. "You can heat water in a cauldron over the stove. I'm sure it's not what you're used to, but . . ."

"Oh, it'll be fine," Millicent assured him. "It'll be nice to rough it for a bit. We're far too mollycoddled at home." She looked at Noah again, as though expecting him to agree with her, but he maintained a stony silence, so she returned her attention to Mr Morrison. "And er . . . what about the . . . other thing?"

Mr Morrison looked at her blankly for a moment and then realised what she was referring to. "Oh . . . you mean . . .? Yes, of course, there's an outhouse around the back," he said.

"An outhouse?" echoed Noah, bewildered.

"He means an outside lavatory," explained Millicent.

"It's er . . . functional, at least," added Mr Morrison. "I'll put a bit of disinfectant down there before I leave."

Millicent nodded. "And you'll be along on Saturday morning to bring more groceries, as arranged?"

"Yes, I'll swing out here first thing."

"Saturday morning?" cried Noah, hoping he'd misheard that last bit. "That's over a week away! What are we supposed to do until then?"

Millicent gave him a long-suffering look. "We'll be fine," she assured him. "I've brought plenty of provisions along, enough to feed an army. I, of course, shall be working on the new book every day in order to meet that deadline. And you..."

"Yes?" he murmured, suspiciously.

"You will be free to explore the island. Think of yourself as my... location manager. I'll give you a list of the kind of places I'm looking for and you can seek them out for me, then note down the routes and so forth. And we'll visit them together in the afternoons."

"Great," said Noah, without enthusiasm.

"This fresh sea air will be very good for both of us," continued Millicent, warming to her theme. "It'll blow away the cobwebs." She had located the box that contained her precious cleaning products and was unpacking its contents onto the table. "Our first job is to get this place cleaned up a bit. Polish the furniture... sweep the floors..."

"I'll get the rest of the luggage from the boat," offered Mr Morrison, turning back towards the door.

"And I'll give you a hand," added Noah hastily and followed the old man outside, telling himself that anything was preferable to the task of swabbing floors. The two of them walked slowly back along the path to the jetty. Ahead of them the grey water looked as flat and as calm as a millpond.

"Something tells me you aren't exactly looking forward to this," said Mr Morrison, giving Noah a sly look.

"I don't understand what she's thinking," muttered Noah. "She used to be able to write anywhere . . . trains . . . hotel rooms . . . deckchairs . . . and now . . ." He shook his head. "Now it's as though she can't make things up anymore. As though she's somehow lost the knack of it." He sighed and then remembered something from their earlier conversation. "You were telling me before . . . about the island's "reputation?" What did you mean by that?"

Mr Morrison looked uncomfortable. "Ach, it was nothing," he said, waving a hand in dismissal. "Like I said, the people out in the sticks can be a superstitious bunch. Sometimes I think they haven't anything better to do than sit around scaring themselves silly. And in a lot of cases, that's no hard thing to achieve." He gave Noah a wink. "It's just . . . stupid talk."

"*What* stupid talk?" insisted Noah. "I wish you'd just tell me."

They had reached the jetty now and their boots clumped hollowly on the weathered wooden boards. Mr Morrison sighed. "Some people . . ." he began; and once again, he hesitated.

"Say it," insisted Noah.

"Some people say the island is haunted," said Mr Morrison.

"Oh, perfect," said Noah.

"You don't want to take any notice though," Mr Morrison assured him. "The ones who say that are the sort who'd think anything out of the ordinary was the result of a curse or bad spirits or whatever. Somebody gets a pimple and it's because a black cat crossed their path on Friday the thirteenth . . . or something equally ridiculous."

"So there's nothing to worry about?"

"Of course not! Why, I've been here scores of times and I've never seen anything out of the ordinary. At least, not in the daylight . . ."

"What are you trying to say? That it's worse at night?"

"No, you're putting words into my mouth. I can assure you that I have never personally seen anything . . ."

"But . . . that means . . . somebody else *has*?"

"Er . . . well . . . it's just that one of the old pals I mentioned . . . a lad by the name of Angus." Mr Morrison chuckled. "Angus McKinnon! Oh, a proper feller-me-lad he was! Some of the stories I could tell you about him, they would fill a book all by themselves." He noticed Noah's exasperated look and attempted to steer the conversation back to the subject at hand. "Well, one time we decided to stay the night on Inchtinn. It was summer and we spread our sleeping bags in the wee cove I pointed out to you. We'd lit a campfire and we were sitting around it telling our stories, trying to spook each other, as young lads do, when . . . Angus became convinced . . . that somebody was . . ."

"Was what?" cried Noah. The old man's hesitations were infuriating.

"He thought that somebody was watching us." Mr Morrison pointed up towards the jagged outline of the crags. "From up there."

Noah turned and looked in the direction he was pointing, thinking about the figure he had glimpsed in the cave mouth only a short while earlier.

"Maybe it was . . . Mr Finlay?" he murmured.

Mr Morrison chuckled. "I hardly think so. We were teenagers. I doubt he was any more than a wee babe in arms when this happened. And like I said, the cabin was an empty wreck in those days. Angus was convinced it was somebody up on the cliff. He wanted to go up there and have a proper look around."

"So did you?"

"At night? Of course not! It would be all too easy to miss your footing up there and fall to your death. There are some treacherous paths. You bear that in mind if you go wandering up there."

"I will. So . . . did you look the next morning?"

"We thought about it."

"And?"

"Well, I'm afraid we had to leave. My father needed his boat back – and he was a man who wouldn't think twice about tanning your backside if you kept him waiting. And besides, by then Angus had convinced himself that it must have been his imagination working overtime. We never spoke of it again."

"Right. So you never found out . . ."

"Oh, hello, looks like your wee friend is back!"

Noah stared at him, bewildered and then turned in the direction he was pointing. The seal had returned. She was bobbing in the water some fifteen feet off shore. Her head was raised and she was gazing intently at Noah, as though she wanted something from him. "She's no friend of mine," murmured Noah.

"I wouldn't be so sure. Looks like she's taken a bit of a shine to you." Mr Morrison winked mischievously. "Maybe she really *is* on the lookout for a new husband." He laughed, clambered down into the boat and began to hand boxes up to Noah, one by one. Noah set them down on the jetty, piling them one atop the other.

"All right," he said. "So it wasn't Mr Finlay. But it could have been whoever did his job before him."

Mr Morrison shook his head. "Finlay is the first one to *have* the job," he said. "Nobody cared about the birds before that. Only about their eggs." He chuckled. "I used to love 'em," he said.

"A couple of those fried and squashed between two rounds of my mother's fresh baked bread." He shook his head, remembering. "There was nothing else like it." He saw the perturbed look on Noah's face and paused for a moment. "What's worrying you, boy?" he asked. "Perhaps I shouldn't have said anything."

"Yes, you should. Only . . . well, I thought when we were coming in just now, I saw somebody up on those rocks."

Mr Morrison shrugged. "Aye, well that *will* have been Finlay," he said. "Spends a lot of time up there. That's where the birds are, you see, in the crags. He has to clamber about to get to the nests. Nothing to worry about." He handed up the last box to Noah and then climbed out onto the jetty. "Right," he said. "We'll start carrying this wee lot up to the cabin, shall we?" He grinned. "If we make enough trips, your mother may have finished cleaning up by the time we're done." He took a large wooden crate in his arms and started back towards the beach. Noah stooped and picked up another box and then hesitated as he heard a sound behind him, a low plaintive bleating. He turned to look and saw that the seal had moved a little closer to the shore. She was gazing at him entreatingly, her black eyes glistening. She opened her mouth and made the noise again and Noah felt a chill go through him, because it sounded almost like a woman crying.

"What do you want?" he asked irritably and then thought how crazy that must sound. He glanced guiltily towards Mr

Morrison but the old man was already some distance away, striding up the beach towards the cabin, whistling tunelessly. Noah returned his gaze to the seal. "I've got nothing for you," he said quietly. "Nothing at all."

The seal gave a last, despairing bleat and sank slowly beneath the surface. Noah caught a glimpse of her speckled flanks drifting silently into the deep, but the image of those glistening eyes remained with him. He shook his head, hefted his box and turning away, he followed Mr Morrison back to the cabin.

Chapter Five

First Night

NOAH SAT ON A WOODEN STOOL AND PEERED through the grimy glass panel of the stove at the flickering orange light of the fire. The long summer day was finally losing its battle with the approaching night. The sun had slipped below the horizon and darkness was spreading across the island like a great impenetrable blanket. A copy of *The Day of the Triffids* lay open on Noah's lap but for the moment at least, he found himself completely unable to look at it. He had felt perfectly comfortable reading the story in his well-lit bedroom at home. But it didn't seem quite so acceptable here, where his mind was already running riot. John Wyndham's descriptions of the weird walking plants, lurching eagerly after their blind victims were enough to make his imagination work overtime.

Behind him, Millicent sat at the pine table, reading through her notes by the light of a hurricane lamp. She had the wind-up gramophone playing in the background, one of her pompous classical pieces. There was no electricity here, so working at night was going to be problematic, but she'd simply announced that she'd get her writing done in the daytime and would use the evenings to "read and relax." Noah couldn't help wondering how anybody was supposed to achieve that in this Godforsaken place. Even though it was midsummer, the cabin felt cold and unwelcoming and he had begged Millicent to allow him to keep the stove running after they had cooked the evening meal, using some of the wood that Mr Morrison had chopped before he left. The meal had comprised a couple of tins of Campbell's tomato soup served with a few cream crackers and Noah reminded himself that there would be two weeks of this kind of diet. It was not an appealing prospect for a boy with a healthy appetite.

Mr Morrison had sailed off in the early afternoon, assuring Millicent that he would return first thing Saturday morning, with boxes of provisions and a few small comforts that she had forgotten to bring along with her and which she had jotted neatly down on a scrap of paper for him.

Noah had walked down to the jetty to see him off. The

old man must have sensed the boy's dread, because he smiled encouragingly and said, "Don't worry, lad, you'll be fine."

"What if something happens?" Noah asked him, bleakly.

Mr Morrison looked puzzled by the question. "Such as?" he asked.

"I don't know. What if . . . well, what if one of us gets ill or something? We won't be able to contact you."

"Of course you will. You'll just have to make your way to Finlay's shack on the far side of the island. He keeps a short wave radio receiver there. He'd give me a call on that and I'd be with you inside the hour. So you see, you're not as cut off as you might suppose."

Noah had taken a little comfort from that. Mr Morrison seemed like the kind of man who kept his word.

"I don't know how to use a short wave radio," he muttered.

"No, but luckily Finlay does." Mr Morrison smiled and took a last look around. "Well, I'll be on my way," he announced. He shook Noah's hand, climbed aboard the dinghy and cast off. Then he leaned over to the outboard motor and got it started. Noah watched dismally as the tiny, ramshackle boat puttered away from the jetty, and slowly dwindled to a speck on the horizon. Noah had an odd feeling then. It seemed to him then that he'd never see the old man again. He grunted, turned away and walked back to the cabin.

Now as the long summer day eased gradually into darkness,

Noah could only hope and pray that maybe on Saturday, Millicent would come to her senses and agree to head back to the mainland with Mr Morrison. Surely she couldn't be enjoying it here? But Noah also knew how stubborn she was. Admitting that she'd made a mistake was not something she ever did lightly.

"Why don't you read your book?" she asked him now, looking up from her notes. "I can get you the other lantern, if you like. We've plenty of paraffin."

He shook his head. "I'm not in the mood for reading," he grunted.

"Well, I can't say I'm surprised. If you will insist on choosing trash like that, you only have yourself to blame."

"It's not trash," he assured her. "It's actually very good."

It irked her that he no longer read *her* books, he realised that and took a perverse kind of pleasure in it. Oh, he had liked them well enough when he was younger but now they seemed somehow trivial to him, these seemingly endless stories about three interfering little busybodies, forever running around discovering smugglers in remote fishing villages or unmasking enemy agents with secret plans to steal somebody's hidden treasures. The problem was that they were all essentially the same story with slight variations. There were other things that irked him. The Adventurers didn't seem to grow any older, which was mystifying, considering all the years that had passed since they first appeared in print . . . and they were always *eating*; wolfing down improbable amounts of sandwiches, cake and sticky buns, without ever putting on so much as an ounce.

"What's so good about Triffids?" Millicent asked him irritably. "It's a nasty little story about death and disaster. I read all the reviews." He knew it was pointless to argue with her about the book. She had already decided that it was in poor taste, this nightmarish story which belonged in a new genre that people were calling "science fiction." She would never understand that Noah wanted to be challenged by what he read – and that after the dark days of the war he needed to be reminded that the world was no longer such an agreeable place.

Millicent pushed her papers aside with a sigh and turned in her seat to look at him. "I thought this trip might be an opportunity for us to talk," she told him. "About what happened at the school."

He sighed. "I already told you what happened," he said, wearily.

"No you didn't. Not in any great detail. The headmaster said that there'd been some kind of an incident at the swimming baths . . . "

Noah laughed at that. "Is that what he called it?" he muttered. "An incident?"

"Yes, and he said that after that, the other boys felt that you didn't want to be with them . . . that you felt somehow . . . superior to them."

"That's not it!" protested Noah. "That's not it at all! I knew they wouldn't understand. It was all Greedo's fault . . ."

"Greedo?"

"Mr Greer, the PT instructor. That's what the boys call him."

"Well, that's charming! Little wonder he has such a dim view of you!"

"I didn't invent the name! Everyone calls him that. It's like a school institution. And anyway, he's perfectly beastly. He tried to make me dive from the high board . . . and he knew it scared me, but he made me do it anyway. I think he enjoys scaring people. And I just . . . panicked, I suppose. And then I thought I was going to drown, so . . ."

But Millicent was shaking her head. "Afraid of the water," she murmured. "I don't know what the Captain would have made of it. He'd be so disappointed."

"Yes, but . . ."

"The water was his *life*. He loved it from childhood, spent every spare minute messing about in boats . . ."

"I know that, but . . ."

"And he introduced you to it, when you were only a little boy. The two of you would go out on the skiff together, you'd sail for miles! He used to tell me that you were a natural sailor. So how did it happen that you became afraid of . . .?"

"I'M NOT HIM!" It came out louder than he'd intended, so loud that it rocked her back in her seat, as though he'd actually punched her. Noah shook his head. "I'm not the Captain," he said again. "And I never will be. And whatever he told you, it's not the truth."

She scowled. "You're suggesting that your father was a liar?" she murmured.

"Of course not! I'm saying he was mistaken. I'm saying he *wanted* to believe that I was like him. But the truth is, I never really enjoyed going out on that skiff with him. Never! He made me do it. He *made* me. And I suppose he thought that eventually I'd grow to like it, but . . . I never did. Every time we went out on the boat, I got a little more scared. The last time we sailed together we were caught in a bad squall and I really thought . . . I thought we were going to die out there. After that I made excuses whenever he asked me to sail with him . . ." He could hardly catch his breath now and he was aware of his vision blurring as his eyes filled with tears. He dashed them dry with the sleeve of his jumper. "I would pretend I was sick or . . . I had schoolwork I needed to finish. It made me feel dreadfully guilty, but I couldn't go with him. I just couldn't!"

Millicent gazed at him for a moment. "You should have said something then," she murmured. "You should have told me."

"When would I have done that?" he cried. "You were always locked up in your study writing your precious books."

Her expression hardened. "Those . . . precious books, as you call them, have paid for a lot of comforts," she told him.

"They've put food on the table, paid for holidays and clothes and nice things to eat. They also paid for those expensive schools you keep getting thrown out of."

"Oh, I wondered when that would come up," he muttered.

She frowned, shook her head. "That came out wrong," she admitted. "I . . . I don't want to fight with you, Noah, I'm just trying to understand what's going on with you. You seem so . . . *nervous* of everything. I wish you could be more confident. I won't always be around and . . ." She broke off at the sound of something outside – a long, shrill cry that seemed to rise on the night air and echo as it died away. Noah looked at her.

"What was that?" he asked quietly.

She shrugged. "Search me," she said. "A bird, I suppose."

"That didn't sound like any bird I've ever heard," he said.

"It'll be an owl or something. I'm sure it's nothing to worry about." She looked at him sternly. "Goodness me, that proves what I was just saying about you! Whatever happened to you to make you so . . . jumpy?"

Noah didn't have an answer to that. He continued to stare at the flickering orange light of the stove, reminding himself that before very much longer, it would be time to head to that unfamiliar little box room and the uncomfortable looking single bed. He would be expected to close his eyes and go to sleep – but he knew only too well that the dream would be waiting for him.

* * *

The skiff pitched and yawed as it headed out over the blustering grey waves. Noah stood in the bow, looking at the way ahead, his eyes straining to see a glimpse of land on the horizon, but it never came. When he glanced anxiously back over his shoulder, there stood the Captain, ramrod straight in his camel-coloured duffle coat, one huge hand gripping the tiller of the boat.

"How much further?" yelled Noah, over the howl of the wind, but the Captain didn't seem to hear him. "Archie? How long before we reach land?"

But the Captain didn't seem to be listening. His steely blue eyes were fixed resolutely on the horizon and it was almost as though he believed he was completely alone on the skiff. As though Noah didn't even exist.

Noah returned his gaze to the way ahead, but the waves were growing ever more turbulent, the horizon shifting and lurching alarmingly as the skiff thundered onwards into the heart of the storm. Noah wanted to suggest that they should turn back, that they should head for calmer water, but somehow he couldn't seem to make the words. And then ahead of them, he saw something huge burst through the surface of the ocean, a great oily head with two expressionless eyes gazing eerily toward the oncoming boat. Noah shouted a warning but his words blew away on the wind and now the head of the beast, whatever it was, rose higher in the water, revealing a set of open jaws, a huge glistening maw from which harp strings of saliva dangled. The skiff rose on a swell and for a moment, the beast was lost to view. Noah hoped it had gone back under the surface . . . but then the boat crested the rise and tipped steeply downwards – and the jaws were waiting far below.

The boat was heading straight towards them and it seemed to Noah that now they resembled the mouth of a gigantic cave.

Noah threw a last frantic look over his shoulder only to see, that, quite unexpectedly, the Captain was gone. Noah was alone on the skiff and it was accelerating downwards into that chasm, fringed with rows of glittering teeth. It was too late to leap clear. Noah could only hang on, transfixed, as the boat shuddered and hurtled headlong into darkness . . .

* * *

He woke with a gasp to find himself lying in the narrow, unfamiliar bed, cold sweat soaking his sheets and pillow. He fought to get his breathing back to normal. It was always the same dream, he'd had it countless times before and it invariably ended the same way, with those mighty jaws closing around him – except that this time, he'd woken a few moments before that could actually happen. He realised that something must have woken him and he didn't know whether to be grateful or concerned.

He sat up and turned his gaze instinctively towards the small, bare window that looked out onto the back of the house. A full moon hung in the night sky, illuminating the overgrown garden and he could make out a tangle of shrubs a short distance from the glass. It seemed to him that there was movement in those shrubs, but he told himself, it was doubtless the result of night winds stirring the foliage. Yes, of course, it had to be that!

But then it occurred to him that one section of the tangle didn't seem to be moving at all and that it appeared to have a smoother outline than the rest. He sat there, staring intently, willing his eyes to come into proper focus and now he was convinced, yes, there *was* an upright shape amidst the restless vegetation, something that seemed completely unaffected by the night wind ... and ... wasn't there an intimation of a cloaked figure standing in the bushes? Wasn't the cowled head of that figure fixed to the dusty glass and staring intently in at him? Couldn't he feel, rather than see, the intensity of a pair of eyes, examining him in every detail? He thought it so calmly that he almost laughed out loud at his own bravado – but then, quite suddenly, the shape moved backwards and to one side, away from the window and it no longer felt like a laughing matter. Noah's breath caught in his throat and almost before he knew it, he was up out of the bed and running for the door, yelling Millicent's name at full volume.

She arrived within minutes, demanding to know what the matter was and he tried to tell her that there had been someone standing at the window, looking in at him, though when he tried to describe exactly what he had seen, he was unable to, because he had seen nothing more than a shadow inside other shadows and the rest had been embroidered by his own imagination.

Of course Millicent told him to go back to bed and to stop being a baby. She said that she'd rig up some kind of a curtain for the window once she could sort out a bit of spare fabric, and she made a point of removing the John Wyndham novel from the chair beside his bed, telling him that he could have it back once he had learned not to let his imagination run away with him.

He went dutifully back to bed, knowing full well that he wasn't going to get any more sleep that night; but though he kept his gaze fixed on the window until the eastern sky finally began to brighten again, there was nothing else to disturb him and nothing to explain what he thought he had seen.

But he was convinced of one thing. Somebody had been watching him – and he needed to know who it was.

Chapter Six

The Cave

BREAKFAST THE FOLLOWING MORNING CONSISTED of badly fried eggs and a rasher of greasy bacon, slapped onto a slice of thickly buttered Hovis. There were also two mugs of sweet tea, made using the new square teabags that had become so popular since the end of the war. Noah and Millicent ate in silence and nothing was said about the previous night's disturbance, but it was evident that she still blamed him for the poor night's sleep she'd had.

Once Noah had rinsed the frying pan and plates under the pump in the back yard, Millicent announced that she was ready to start work and settled herself at the kitchen table. When Noah asked what she thought he might do to occupy his time, she suggested that he should go and look for the track down to the beach that Mr Morrison had mentioned, because it was another lovely day and she might just fancy a dip later on.

Noah knew better than to argue. He left her tapping furiously at her portable typewriter and headed out along the path that led past the wooden outhouse, across the scrawny stretch of overgrown garden and away towards the cliffs. In the daylight, Inchtinn seemed a much more agreeable place. The track swung to the right over a short stretch of moorland and then rose dramatically upwards through a narrow gap in some boulders. Very soon, it had turned into a steep ascent, the grey basalt rocks on either side of him becoming ever more jagged; and then ahead of him he saw birds, large white gulls, most of them nesting on the ground amongst the boulders. As he passed near a huddled pair, one of them lifted its head and gave out a long, echoing shriek. Noah realised that this was the sound he and Millicent had heard the previous night and felt a little reassured.

He walked onwards and noticed that some of the birds seemed to be becoming more agitated by the moment, flapping upwards into the air as he went by and in some cases even swooping low over his head, as though trying to warn him off, but he held his nerve and pretty soon, he crested a rise and saw the sea perhaps a hundred feet below him. He could hear the sound of waves pounding on an unseen shore. He paused for a moment and moved closer to the edge so he could take a proper look – and sure enough, there was the track, zig-zagging its way downwards to the same cove that Mr Morrison has pointed out on their way in. From this height, it looked like an inviting little oasis almost completely enclosed by sheer grey rock. He was about to start down the path to make a more detailed inspection but something made him turn his head and look to his left. He frowned, as he saw, in the face of a row of sheer crags, the open mouth of a cave and for an instant, his mind filled with an image from his dream of the previous night; that of the sea beast's open jaws waiting to swallow him – but then he remembered that he thought he'd glimpsed a figure standing in what surely must have been the same cave mouth when the boat was approaching the jetty, yesterday morning. Against his better judgement, he turned aside from the track and began to scramble his way across an uneven scatter of stones and boulders, towards the cave.

As he drew closer, the sun slipped behind the looming cliff face and a chill settled around him. He hesitated for a moment, wondering if he was doing the right thing, but something made him keep going. He reached the mouth of the cave and peered apprehensively inside. He saw that there was a flat, pebbly floor in there, above which rock caverns arched dramatically. He could only see a short distance into the opening before things dissolved into darkness and he thought about abandoning the quest and returning to the brighter, more welcoming pleasures of the cove with its white sand beach. But then he had a mental image of Millicent's mocking expression, and heard her voice chiding him for being such a "nervous boy" and something within him bristled. He decided that he would show her a thing or two – that he could be just as adventurous as her fictional hero, Douglas, when he put his mind to it. He drew in a breath, took a cautious step into the cave. Nothing untoward happened, so he took another – and then another.

Once inside, the sound seemed to change altogether. The restless whoosh of the surf hundreds of feet below was suddenly muted and replaced by the sound of unseen water dripping into a pool. He moved slowly forward, keeping his eyes fixed to the ground, nervous of tripping on a rock and bashing his head, but the floor appeared to be pretty level in here – and then he noticed what looked like the remains of an old campfire over against one wall, large flat rocks arranged in a circle. He went over and crouched beside it, wondering how recently it might have been used. In the uncertain light, he saw that there were ashes in the bottom of a shallow pit, which had long since turned to fine powder. He even put the tips of his fingers into them, to see if there was any warmth there, something that Douglas had done in one of the Adventurers books, but decided that nobody had used this recently, maybe not even in years.

He was about to stand up when something else caught his eye, something half-buried in the ash. He reached out and pulled it free, then turned it around in his hands. It was a conical seashell, the kind that the Captain had once told him was called a conch, not the huge sort you sometimes saw, but about the size of a chocolate eclair. Noah brushed some of the ash from it and then spat on it and wiped it with his fingers, revealing that it was brilliantly coloured under the grey coating, a pale cream marked with vivid red and yellow splashes. He stood up and carried the conch a few steps back towards the cave mouth so he could examine it in more detail and now he was intrigued, because he could see that somebody had made a row of four little holes in a straight line along its length. The holes were evenly spaced, too regular to have been caused by a natural occurrence. It was almost like . . .

He noticed how the four holes coincided with the tips of his fingers, reminding him of an old ocarina he'd had when he was little – and he noticed also, how the open end of the conch looked exactly like a mouthpiece. Almost before he knew what he was doing, he had lifted it to his lips and was blowing into it, producing a clear, pure note that seemed to echo around the interior of the cave. He took his lips away with a gasp of delight and then, placing his fingertips onto the holes, he raised it to his mouth again and blew a longer blast of air, experimenting by lifting his fingers, one by one. Sure enough, the conch produced four different notes, a simple musical scale. Noah chuckled, delighted with his discovery and tried to remember one of the little tunes he had been taught when he was a child. What was an easy one to play? Ah, yes, *Three Blind Mice!* Now, how did that go? He attempted to reproduce it, got a couple of the notes wrong at first, but tried a different combination and suddenly, it came back to him and he remembered exactly how to play it. He went through the phrase a couple of times, getting more confident with each attempt.

"*Three blind mice. Three Blind Mice. See how they run. See how they ...*"

He broke off in surprise as he thought he became aware of movement at the back of the cave. He turned to look, straining his eyes to see into the shadows . . . and was reminded of the previous evening, how he had thought there was somebody standing just outside his bedroom window . . .

"H . . . hello?" he called, and was momentarily startled when his voice echoed eerily back to him. "Who . . . who's there?"

There was no reply – but he thought he heard *something*, perhaps the sound of somebody letting out a slow breath in the darkness. He slipped the conch into his pocket and took an exploratory step deeper into the cave.

"Hello?" he called. "Is there somebody . . .?"

"Hey! Who's that?"

The commanding voice came from behind Noah, making him spin around with a gasp of surprise. A man was standing in the cave mouth, silhouetted against the light, his hands on his hips. "Come out of there where I can see you."

Noah didn't feel inclined to argue. He stumbled closer to the entrance and stepped out into the light. The middle-aged man regarding him was thin and wiry, his face largely obscured by a dark grey beard. He was dressed in a khaki jacket and trousers, his feet encased in rugged walking boots. He carried a canvas rucksack on his back and Noah thought that he looked to be equipped for climbing Everest rather than walking along a row of crags. Noah also decided that it was obvious who this was.

"You must be Mr Finlay," he said.

The man's dark eyes narrowed suspiciously. "That's right," he growled. "And who are you, if you don't mind me asking?"

"I'm Noah McCallum." Noah extended a hand, as Millicent had always taught him to do when encountering a stranger. "I'm staying at the cabin with my Mother." He jerked a thumb over his shoulder to give a general idea of the direction he had come from. "We'll be there for a couple of weeks."

"Will you now?" Mr Finlay didn't seem to be overjoyed at this information, but he took Noah's hand and gave it a brief shake. The hand was rough and calloused, Noah noticed, and exerted a more powerful grip than was necessary. "How d'you know who I am?" The man's accent wasn't that dissimilar to Mr Morrison's, but Noah thought, nothing like as warm.

"Oh, er . . . it's just that Mr Morrison mentioned you. He said you were the only other person on the island, so . . ."

Mr Finlay grunted. "Morrison? That old reprobate still taking money off the unwary, is he?"

"Umm . . ." Noah wasn't sure what Mr Finlay meant by this, so he just smiled. "He told us you watch the birds here," he added.

"I do more than just *watch* them, sonny," said Mr Finlay, sounding quite annoyed. "I *study* them. I protect them. I write reports about them for my employers on the mainland." He looked at Noah intently. "There was a time when people thought they could come over here and help themselves to eggs," he said and somehow managed to make it sound like an accusation. "Most of the females are guarding clutches right now," he said. "You need to be careful, young man. They can be quite aggressive when they put their wee minds to it."

Noah nodded. "Yes, one or two of them flew quite low over my head on the way up here."

Mr Finlay chuckled. "I bet they did! Ach, but that's nothing! I've known some of those aggressive males swoop down and go for people's eyes, before now. You need to watch yourself." He seemed to think for a moment. "So, you're staying in the old Crannach cabin, are you?"

"I . . . suppose so. What's a 'crannach'?"

Mr Finlay chuckled mirthlessly. "That's the name of the auld fellow who last lived there. A hermit, by all accounts." He smiled unpleasantly. "He went mad and killed himself." He noted Noah's look of alarm and seemed to relish it. "This was many years ago, of course."

"Why . . . why would he do a thing like that?" croaked Noah.

Mr Finlay shrugged. "How would I know? I never met him. I only know what I heard – that he was away with the fairies . . ."

"I'm sorry, I don't under . . ."

"He was addled in the head. That's what people say, anyway. It's no great surprise really, stuck out here all by himself, day after day, with nothing to do but brood on his own misfortune." He nodded his head towards the ridge of rocks behind him. "Threw himself off that cliff, he did, onto the rocks below. Made a terrible mess. And of course, he wasn't found for months, so there wasn't much left of him to bury." He grinned ghoulishly.

Noah swallowed. "But . . . *you* live here by yourself, don't you?"

Mr Finlay looked surprised, as though he hadn't thought of that. "Well, aye, of course, but . . . *I* have things to occupy me," he said, sounding defensive. "I have the birds. By all accounts, Crannach had nothing in his life. Well, nothing but the past. He was obsessed with the history of the island – the terrible things that happened here over the years."

Noah opened his mouth to ask what they might be but Mr Finlay cut him off with a question. "What were you doing in the cave just now?" he asked. "When I was coming up the path, I thought I heard you talking to somebody."

"Oh . . ." Noah glanced back into the dark maw of the cave. "It was just that . . . I thought there was somebody hanging around in there."

Mr Finlay gave him an odd look. "Nobody goes in there," he said.

"But . . ." Noah frowned. "Didn't I spot *you* in there? Yesterday morning, when our boat was coming in to the jetty?"

Mr Finlay shook his head. "Not me," he said. "No, I would have been back at my hut, writing up reports. I certainly wouldn't have been in the cave. Like I said, most people give that place a wide berth."

"Why do they do that?" asked Noah, nervously, but Mr Finlay seemed to ignore the question.

"You must have imagined it," he concluded.

Noah nodded, but he was unconvinced. He was pretty sure he'd seen *somebody* standing in the cave mouth yesterday – and he was also pretty sure he'd heard movement just a few moments earlier. "Mr Morrison said you have a hut," he said. "Where exactly *is* it?"

Mr Finlay pointed along the treacherous looking path that led along the cliff top. "You just follow this track here until you find yourself going past the old leper hospital up on the cliff top," he said. "After a while, the path starts to decline again and eventually you come to my place. You can't really miss it." Again, his eyes narrowed. "Why are you so interested?"

"Oh, it's just that my mother said that she wouldn't mind having a chat with you some time?"

"Your mother?"

"Yes. She writes children's books, you see and . . ."

Mr Finlay made a kind of scoffing sound. "Some kind of hobby, I suppose?"

"Oh no, she's rather good at it. You may have heard of her."

Mr Finlay looked doubtful. "I don't read children's books," he said.

"No, of course you don't. But she *is* quite well known." He wasn't sure why, but he felt he wanted to impress this rather dismissive man who he'd only just met. "Millicent Palmer?" he ventured. "She writes *The Adventurers* and . . ."

"I thought you said your name was McCallum?"

"Oh, yes, well that was my father's name. My mother goes by Palmer. Millicent Palmer?" He tried again. "She's really is rather well known."

"Not to me, I'm afraid." Mr Finlay shrugged. "Well, you're welcome to call around, either of you, though I can't say when I'll be home to receive visitors. I'm kept quite busy. Especially during the nesting season." He frowned, looked at his boots for a moment. "And if you do decide to come, don't be expecting much. It's very Spartan. Tiny, really."

"How come you don't use our cabin?" Noah asked him. "When we're not there, I mean? Mr Morrison said it's bigger than your place."

Mr Finlay gave Noah an odd look. "Oh, I wouldn't want to be staying there," he said. "I mean, it's a free world and everything but . . . no, that wouldn't do for me at all. Too much baggage." He seemed to remember something. "Anyway, I have to be on my way now. Things to do." He gave Noah a stern look. "You watch out for those birds, lad. Especially the guillemots. They can be very fierce."

And with that, he turned away and started to stride along the narrow track, placing his feet with the kind of confidence that only comes with regular practice. Noah watched him until he was lost to sight. Then he turned his head and looked back into the cave, thinking about going in there a second time – but then he remembered something he'd glimpsed earlier amongst the jumble of equipment that Millicent had brought with her – the Captain's old Eveready torch, powered by a carbide battery. Maybe, he told himself, he'd borrow that and come back tomorrow for a more detailed look.

For now, he'd go and see what the beach had to offer. He made his way carefully down the path, taking his time, because parts of it were very precarious, skirting steep drops onto jagged stone. Just before he reached the level ground that edged the beach, he turned and looked back up at the cliff that now reared up against the blue sky behind him.

There was the cave mouth – and just for an instant, he thought that once again, he glimpsed movement in the shadow of it, a small, slight figure ducking backwards into deeper cover.

"Who *are* you?" he murmured to himself, but decided now was not the time to find out. *But soon*, he thought. *Very soon*. He turned away and continued walking towards the cove.

Chapter Seven

On the Beach

HE STROLLED SLOWLY OUT ACROSS THE EXPANSE of white sand and it was, he decided, like stepping into another world. With high walls of curving basalt on either side of him, the sheer cliffs behind and the restless sea directly ahead, it felt to Noah as though he was completely cut off from the rest of the island. Even the sight of the waves breaking onto the shore ahead of him didn't fill him with his usual sense of apprehension. Shielded from the wind, he was aware of the warm, soothing touch of sunlight on his face.

On impulse, he reached down, pulled off his shoes and

socks and strolled barefoot to the water's edge, relishing the feel of the warm sand beneath the soles of his feet. Shielding his eyes with the flat of one hand, he gazed out across leagues of swaying water and could just make out a hazy grey outline on the horizon; the mainland. He found himself wondering if the distance was swimmable. It had taken Mr Morrison something like fifty minutes to make the crossing in the boat. A strong swimmer could probably do it in a couple of hours, he decided – but the thought of it once again reminded him of the dream, those terrible gaping jaws opening to receive him. He shivered. He knew there were no sea monsters out there and yet . . . standing on this beach, gazing out over the ocean, he somehow felt that there *could* be.

He tilted back his head and noted a few solitary birds high above him, wheeling and soaring on the air. Gulls? Or guillemots? Those were the ones that Mr Finlay had warned him about, but he hadn't the faintest idea what a guillemot looked like. Whatever they were, the ones above him seemed to be taking absolutely no notice of him. He sighed. Millicent was going to love this place, he thought. Of course, she would urge him to take a dip with her and naturally, he would have to say no – but he thought he might just be brave enough to do a bit of paddling in the shallows . . .

He was about to turn away when something broke the surface of the water with an abrupt splash, startling him. Somehow he wasn't surprised to see the seal's comical whiskered head rearing up from the water. It was the same one, he was pretty sure of that. She had a distinctive white mark just above one of those impossibly appealing black eyes – eyes that were staring intently at Noah once again, as though seeking something from him. He spread his hands in a gesture of helplessness.

"I already told you, I've got nothing for you," he said and once again, felt ridiculous for talking to a creature that couldn't possibly answer back. But happily there was nobody else here to hear him this time. The seal held her position and gave an anxious little bleat – and Noah could understand how the legend of the selkie must have come about in the first place, because it really did sound almost human.

"What do you want?" he asked and the seal seemed to react to the sound of his voice. She reared up in the water, then came down with a splash and disappeared from sight. For a moment, he was aware of her form, gliding beneath the surface like a phantom and then she was gone. Noah shook his head. Talking to a seal. What next? There was surely no hope for him. He turned to his left to study the wall of basalt that edged that side of the beach, noticing that there were many little nooks and openings in the stone and curious, he walked in that direction to have a closer look.

Something caught his eye. In one crevice, a few feet from the ground, somebody had chiselled a row of large words into the rock. They were poorly defined, as though they had been inscribed a long time ago, their sharp edges worn smooth by years of wind and rain. Noah crouched down and traced the five words with the tip of an index finger.

GOD HAVE MERCY ON US

He frowned. It seemed a desperate thing for somebody to have left in such a tranquil setting. Why would anyone have taken the trouble to do it? His gaze moved downwards from the message and he noticed a scatter of shells lining the edge where stone and sand met. This made him remember something. The conch! He had slipped it into his pocket when he'd thought he heard a sound at the back of the cave. He reached in and took the shell out again, examined it in the daylight. It really was a handsome thing, he decided, the colours even more vibrant in the sunshine. He wondered who had made it and why they had left it in the fireplace. For some reason, he had the conviction that it hadn't been left recently – that it had probably lain there for a long time. He raised the conch to his mouth again and played *Three Blind Mice*, but out in the open air it lacked the eerie appeal of the way it had sounded in the cave, all echoey and spectral. He returned the conch to his pocket, deciding that he would hang on to it for the time being. He could always return it later if he decided that somebody might come looking for it.

He stood upright and walked back across the beach to examine the far side, but though he spent some time looking, he found nothing of any great interest there, just more broken shells, a couple of dead crabs and an old wooden pallet that must have drifted ashore at some point over the years; so he decided that perhaps it was probably time to head back to the cabin. He retraced his steps to the place where he had cast off his shoes and socks, sat down in the sand and pulled them on again. Grains of sand felt scratchy between his toes.

He stood up, turned around and headed back the way he had come, climbing laboriously up the steep slope that led back to the cliff top. He had gone only a short distance when something stopped him in his tracks – an urgent calling sound. He turned to look and saw to his amazement that the seal had returned. Now she was actually up on the beach, just past the waterline. She was moving back and forth on her flippers, calling out in apparent agitation, as though begging him not to leave. He couldn't help smiling and he thought about what Mr Morrison had told him about selkies.

"I'm too young to get married!" he called and she stopped moving and stared straight back at him, her expression mournful. He laughed delightedly, turned away and scrambled onwards up the slope. The next time he looked back there was no sign of her. She must have finally taken the hint, he told himself. He reached the top of the ridge and stood for a moment, gazing at the cave mouth away to his right. He moved closer, debating whether or not he should go back for another look, but decided, no, he'd wait until he had the torch. Then he could go in there and study it properly. He stared into those stygian depths but could no longer sense any movement. Perhaps, he told himself, he was only imagining that somebody was crouched in the shadows, watching him, but for some reason, he shouted into the darkness.

"Whoever's in there . . . I'll be back!" His voice echoed and he stood for a moment, wondering what had possessed him to call out like that. Perhaps this was how Mr Crannach got started, he thought and chuckled at the idea; but then he remembered what Mr Finlay had told him about the old man's death and really didn't feel it was all that funny. Still, it would make an interesting story for Millicent – *if* he decided to share it with her.

And with that, he turned away and strode back along the trail that took him gradually downhill to the back garden of the cabin.

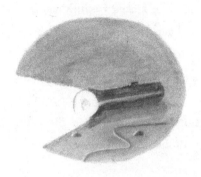

Chapter Eight

Inspiration

HE CAME IN AT THE FRONT DOOR, FULLY EXPECTING to find Millicent still hammering industriously away on her typewriter, but she was sitting at the table staring abstractedly into space and Noah couldn't help noticing a pile of scrunched up sheets of paper by her feet. Not a good sign, he decided.

"Everything all right?" he asked her warily.

She turned to look at him, a glum expression on her face. "It's not coming," she said tonelessly.

"What's not coming?" he asked, baffled.

"Inspiration." She kicked fretfully at one of the balls of paper. It skittered across the floor towards Noah. He bent and picked it up, started to carefully unfold it.

"Don't bother reading that," she warned him. "It's no good at all."

But he ignored her and studied the paragraph she had typed before becoming so disheartened.

It was a fine July morning and the Adventurers were bored. They sat around Grandma Pearson's little cottage, sipping tea and eating ginger biscuits. It was only the second week of the school holidays. During the first week they had been all over the local area, in search of something new, but so far, had found nothing of any interest.

"There must be somewhere we haven't visited yet!" complained Douglas.

"We could take the skiff out again," suggested Sally, trying to be helpful. "It's a lovely day for sailing."

"But where would we go?" asked Harriet. We've been *everywhere*!"

Just then Grandma Pearson came in to the room. She had clearly been listening in to

their conversation. "I can think of one place
you've never been," she said mysteriously.
"The Island."

    "The Island?" cried Douglas. "Where's
that?"

It was all Millicent had written before tearing the sheet
from the typewriter and crumpling it up. "What's wrong with
this?" asked Noah. "It sounds pretty much like all your other
stories."

"That's just the point," muttered Millicent. "I don't *want*
this to be like all the others. I want to do something different,
this time."

He frowned. "Are you allowed to?" he asked her.

"What do you mean?" she snapped. "Of course I'm allowed
to! I can write whatever I like."

Noah carried the paper back to the table and set it down
beside the typewriter. "Yes, but . . . it can't be *too* different, can
it? I mean, surely your readers expect you to write a certain
way, so . . ."

Millicent stood up from the table and went over to the
window. "You're as bad as Alicia," she complained. "Perhaps
you should consider becoming a literary agent yourself. You
seem to have the right disposition for it."

"Why, has *she* been telling you how to write?"

"Not exactly. At least, not in so many words. But she *loves* to point out what she calls "interesting new trends.""

"What, you mean like science fiction?" he offered, trying not to smile.

She gave a dismissive snort. "You won't catch me writing that kind of nonsense," she told him. "I do have some standards." She made a dismissive gesture. "How did you get on?" she asked. "Did you find the beach?"

"Yes. It was easy enough. You just follow the track and eventually you come to it. Oh, I also spoke to that Mr Finlay."

Millicent turned away from the window, looking very interested. "Did you indeed? And what's he like, pray tell?"

Noah scowled. "He's all right, I suppose. A bit . . ." He wasn't sure how to say exactly what he meant. "He wasn't very friendly. But he said we're both welcome to pay him a visit some time."

"Hmm. Well, I might just take him up on that. You never know, he might spark off some new ideas." She studied the typewriter for a few moments. "What was the beach like?"

"Nice. A bit of a suntrap. I'm sure you'll like it." He smiled, remembering something. "That seal was there again. You know, the one we saw from the boat? It was strange, because she kept calling out to me. Almost as though she was trying to tell me something."

Millicent chuckled mischievously. "Perhaps Mr Morrison

was right about her. Maybe she *has* got her eye on you."

"Well, she's come to the wrong person," said Noah. "I'm not looking to settle down just yet. Is there anything to eat?" he added.

Millicent nodded to the pile of cardboard boxes stacked up beside the window. "You'll find bread in the top box – and there's butter and a pot of jam in one of the others. Why not make yourself a sandwich? I expect you can manage that, can't you?"

"Of course. Shall I make one for you while I'm at it?"

She shook her head. "I'm not in the least bit hungry," she said. "You know, I think I might go down to the beach for a swim."

"I thought you were anxious to hit your deadline?"

"Oh, don't be such a slave driver!"

"It's not me who's doing the slave-driving. That's Alicia's job."

"Yes, but I'd say you'd make a good little apprentice for her. Perhaps that's an area you should be looking towards after school. Proof reading, copy editing, that kind of thing. You could help me with my books."

He rolled his eyes. "Oh yes, I'm sure you'd take my criticisms on board."

Millicent leaned back in her chair and massaged the small of her back. She let out a soft groan. "Perhaps a dip in the ocean *would* help get my imagination working," she said.

He picked up the topmost box and carried it to the other end of the pine table. He took out a breadboard, the loaf and a knife and busied himself cutting off a couple of thick slices. "You never used to have these problems," he observed. "I remember you telling me once that you could write anywhere."

She looked wistful now as though his remark had stirred memories she didn't care to dwell on. "That was then," she said, briskly. "A lot of things have changed since those days. You'll learn as you get older, Noah, that nothing ever stays the same. I thought your father and I would be together forever, but that didn't exactly go as planned. Along came that damned war and everything that mattered went straight out of the window. "Your country expects every man to do his duty!" And that was that . . . he was gone and I was a war widow . . . Goodness me, Noah, go easy with that butter! It's supposed to last us a week!"

"Sorry." Noah located a jar of strawberry jam and spooned some onto one slice of bread, then spread it with a knife. He slapped the other slice on top and he had a doorstop sandwich. He carried it over to the end of the table and settled into the spare seat opposite Millicent. He took an enormous bite and chewed noisily. "Do you think we've brought enough food?" he asked, his mouth full.

"I'm already beginning to wonder," she said, disparagingly. "If you carry on at that rate, we won't last two days."

"Well, I suppose if we look to be in danger of running out, we can always call for Mr Morrison to bring more."

Millicent looked puzzled. "How would we do that exactly? He isn't going to be able to hear us from this distance, is he?"

Noah chuckled. "No, not that sort of call! Mr Finlay has a short wave radio. Mr Morrison told me. We can contact him on that."

"I see . . ." Millicent seemed irritated at this news. "It would have been jolly useful if he'd told *me* that. Why do people always assume the little woman doesn't need to know anything? But they'll happily give the information to a fourteen-year-old boy. They . . ." She suddenly looked abstracted.

"Something wrong?" asked Noah.

"No. But I was just thinking . . . maybe I should give Douglas a radio set. He's the sort who could put a thing like that to good use. It would be quite a handy piece of equipment for him."

She was always talking like this, as though Douglas was a real person who she could make a gift to. Noah was well used to it.

"Oh, yes, and then he could use it in the story, I suppose."

"Hmm. If I could somehow weave it into the plot . . . how exactly do you use a short wave radio?"

Noah shrugged. "Search me. I expect Mr Finlay can tell you," he said.

"Hmm. Another reason to seek him out." She stood up from her chair and started towards the door of her room. "I think I'll go and put on my swimming togs," she said. "And I'll head down to the beach. Are you going to come with me?"

He was about to tell her, no, that he'd just walked back from there; but then the image of the cave mouth filled his head and he said, "Yes, why not?"

"Excellent. I packed your trunks, they'll be in the small suitcase."

"Oh, I'm not going to swim," he reminded her.

"No, but you'll need to be properly attired, even if you're just splashing about in the shallows."

"Yes, I suppose so."

He waited until Millicent had gone into the other room and then got up from his seat and went over to the pile of boxes by the window. He rooted through them, until he found the Captain's old torch. He tried the button, just to make sure the battery was working and when he saw that it was, he slipped the torch into his pocket and went back to the table to finish his sandwich.

* * *

Fifteen minutes later, he and Millicent were heading back uphill, Millicent carrying a canvas bag over one shoulder, which held her towel, her sunhat and a paperback romance. As they walked, Noah pointed out the various things he'd encountered on his previous trip. Pretty soon, they saw the nesting birds, ahead of them. One or two of them flapped upwards into the air and started circling threateningly above their heads, but Millicent treated them with casual disdain, simply waving her arms to scare them away if one of them got a little too close for comfort.

"Mr Finlay said we had to watch out for the guillemots," Noah warned her. "Though I haven't the faintest idea which ones they are. He said something about them going for your eyes."

Millicent looked unimpressed. "It'll take more than a few seagulls to scare me off," she assured Noah. "And it sounds to me as if Mr Finlay has been reading too much Daphne Du Maurier."

Noah gave her a puzzled look. "I don't understand," he said.

"Oh, she just published a ghastly short novel about birds attacking people. Absolutely horrible. I've no doubt she and your Mr Wyndham would be perfect companions for each other."

"Why do you hate him so much?" asked Noah.

"It's not *him*, so much as what he represents – a total breakdown of morality. I had thought that Daphne was better than that. She's done some lovely romance novels in the past, but lately she seems to be becoming ever more lurid." She paused for a moment, as if feeling tired. "Is it much further?" she asked.

"No. Once we get to the top of the hill, you'll be able to see the beach."

She nodded. "I mustn't make too much of a habit of this," she said. "Before I know it the two weeks will be up and I've absolutely promised Alicia that I'll have that new manuscript for her just as soon as I get back."

Noah gave her a quizzical look. "But it's not as if it *has* to be ready, is it?" he reasoned. "I mean, if it takes a little longer, then it does. She can't make you write if you don't feel like it."

Millicent looked outraged. "It's a matter of professionalism," she said. "I promised her it will be ready and I can't go back on my word. That's simply not the way I do things."

"No, of course not, but . . ."

"Oh, look at it!" They had finally reached the top of the ridge and were gazing down at the secluded cove, which in the full light of midday looked even more inviting than it had earlier. Millicent started immediately down the descent.

"Watch your step," Noah warned her. "It's a bit tricky in places."

"Oh, don't fuss!" Millicent's gaze was focused on the cove and for some reason, as they started down, Noah didn't draw her attention to the cave mouth away to their left. He realised it was only a matter of time before she *did* notice it, but part of him wanted to keep it to himself for as long as possible. They made their way steadily down the rocky incline, until they finally reached the expanse of white sand. Once there, Millicent took a blanket from her shoulder bag, unrolled it and laid it out. She removed her outer layers to reveal that she was wearing a black bathing suit underneath. That was when Noah made his excuse.

"Oh, I forgot to bring my trunks!" he exclaimed

She gave him a look of disbelief. "Noah, I specifically reminded you to get them before we left! I assumed you had them on under your trousers."

"Yes, I'm sorry, I completely forgot. No problem, I'll just nip back for them."

"Really? Can you be bothered?"

"Yes, it won't take me long. You relax and I'll be here before you know it."

"All right, then. Be careful climbing those rocks."

"Oh, don't fuss!" he said, mimicking her own earlier remark but she missed the dig completely. She was settling herself down on the towel and placing a wide-brimmed straw hat on her head, gazing out to sea, as though mesmerised by the sight of it.

Noah retraced his steps, reaching into his pocket to make sure the torch was still there. At the top of the incline, he glanced back to ensure that Millicent wasn't watching him, but she was still gazing out towards the horizon, no doubt thinking of the best way she might incorporate a short wave radio into her story. Noah veered to his right and climbed the last rocky incline up to the mouth of the cave. He paused by the entrance a moment and peered inside, then took a couple of steps into the semi-darkness, taking out the torch as he did so.

"I'm back already," he announced into the darkness and even though he had expected it, was still startled by the sound of his voice echoing out at him. He stopped for a moment to listen and thought he heard a soft movement off in the shadows, away to his left. "I don't know who you are, but I don't think it's polite to be creeping around in the dark. Was it you who was peeping in my bedroom window last night?" The echo of the question hung on the air, unanswered. Noah scowled. "Why don't you come over and introduce yourself?" he asked. Again, he listened and told himself no, he wasn't imagining it. There was the sound again, a soft intake of breath. Somebody was standing a short distance off to his left hand side, he was sure of it now – but it was evident that whoever was there, didn't want to say anything to give themselves away. In the darkness, Noah's mouth curved into a smile as he anticipated the surprise that whoever was there was about to get.

"All right," he said. "If that's how you want to play this . . ."

He lifted his right hand, aimed the torch in what he thought was the right direction. Then he pressed the button and the torchlight blazed.

Chapter Nine

Coira

"**P**LEASE STOP!" IT WAS A FEMALE VOICE, NOAH decided and it sounded so desperate, so terrified, that he reacted instinctively, flicking the torch off again. He stood there in the darkness, mouth open, his heart thumping in his chest as he processed what he had just seen. In the brief instant in which he'd been able to view her, the girl on the far side of the cave had been reacting as though the torchlight was actually burning her. Noah had registered an image of a cloaked and hooded figure, scuttling away from the light, holding up one hand to shield her face from the glare . . . oh, and there had been one other thing. He'd noticed that something was terribly wrong with that upraised hand.

He listened intently and could hear her gasping now, as though still afraid. "I'm . . . I'm sorry," he said. "I didn't mean to scare you."

"What was that?" came her voice. "The light! It burned my eyes!"

"Oh, it's only a torch," he said. "I just wanted to see you, that's all."

"I cannot take the light. It hurts." The voice was Scottish, he decided, a hard-edged guttural accent of a kind he had never heard before, quite unlike the ones used by Mr Morrison and Mr Finlay. "I can still see it," said the girl's voice. "In wee circles dancing before me."

"Oh, it just . . . dazzled you," he assured her. "It will pass in a few moments."

"Ah, good. That's good." There was more laboured breathing, but she sounded a little calmer now.

"Who . . . who are you?" he asked the darkness.

A short pause. Then: "I am Coira."

"Coira?" He frowned. It wasn't a name he had ever heard before. "What . . . what are you doing here?" he asked.

"I live here," said the voice.

"On Inchtinn?"

"In this cave."

He almost did a double take on that. Who lived in a cave in this day and age? Well, somebody called Coira, by all accounts.

"I don't understand," he said.

"What is *your* name?" asked the girl's voice.

"Me? I'm Noah."

"Ah . . ." A slow breath. "Coira . . . and, Noah. Our names are . . . alike."

"I suppose they are a bit . . . look, could you perhaps come a little closer? It feels strange talking to somebody I can't actually see."

"You won't . . . make the light again?"

Strange way of putting it, thought Noah. *Make the light.* "No," he said. "Not if you don't want me to. Just . . . come closer where I can see you. Please?"

There was a very long pause then, but finally he was aware of movement. And then he could just discern the hooded shape of her, shuffling cautiously nearer, until she was standing some ten feet away. He still couldn't make out any details. She wore a shapeless hooded cloak, which was pulled tight around her and the hood hung low over her face, obscuring her features. Her hands were now completely covered by long, loose-fitting sleeves.

"Are you . . . in some kind of trouble?" asked Noah. He wasn't sure why he had asked that, but he couldn't imagine why else she might be hiding away in a remote place like this.

"No. No, I'm fine. They are going now . . ."

"They?"

"The circles of light."

"Oh. That's good . . ." He cast around for something else to say. "This will probably sound strange," he murmured. "But . . . were you . . . I mean, were you looking in my bedroom window last night?"

A long soft sigh but no answer.

"I thought I saw somebody standing in the bushes, looking in . . . somebody wearing a . . . sorry, is that a coat you're wearing or a . . . a cloak?"

Again, she made no reply, so he decided it might be better to change the subject. He thought for a moment. "Did you . . . mean what you just said? That you live in this cave."

"Aye. I live quietly. I keep myself to myself. I do not harm anyone. I . . . I don't think this cave belongs to anybody, so I really don't think it matters . . . unless, perhaps, it is your cave?"

"No, don't be silly! I'm just a visitor. But . . . how long have you been staying here? I mean . . . it's a *cave*! Where do you sleep?"

"I do not sleep," said the girl.

He stared at her figure in the half-light. "Well, that's ridiculous," he said. "You *must* sleep! Everybody has to sleep!"

The cowled head shook from side to side but she didn't say anything else on that subject.

"And . . . what about food?"

"What about it?"

"Well, I mean to say, what do you eat? Do you want me to bring you anything? Food, water . . .?"

"No. Thank you. I do not need them."

He actually laughed at that. He was starting to think that somebody was playing a joke on him. "Look," he told her. "I tell you what. My mother's just a short distance from here, on the beach. Perhaps I should fetch her and . . ."

"NO!" The single word spoken at a volume that echoed around the interior of the cave, made him jump. "No, nobody else must see me. I cannot allow it. I only came to you because you . . . summoned me."

"Did I?" Now he really was bewildered. "I don't think so."

"Yes. You played my shell!"

"Your . . ." He realised what she was referring to, reached into his pocket and pulled out the conch. He held it out to her. "This?" he cried. "This is yours?"

The hooded head nodded briefly.

"Oh, I'm sorry, I had no idea it belonged to somebody. It was just lying around. Here . . ." He took a step forward to hand the conch back to her, but she backed quickly away. "Please, stay where you are!" she said.

He stopped in his tracks. "I don't mean you any harm," he assured her. "I just wanted to give this back to you."

"No, you keep that. I have no use for it now."

"But didn't you just say it was yours?" He looked at the

conch in his hand, noting the carefully made holes along its surface. "Did you . . . did you make this?" he asked.

"Aye."

"Only, it looks . . . really old."

Another of those strange sighs escaped her. "It was . . . a long time ago," she said, and there was a desperate sadness in the way she said it, as though she was thinking about something in the past.

"I found it earlier. It was half-buried . . . in the ashes of a fire."

"Aye. That's right."

"So you . . . threw it away?"

"Something like that."

Once again there was a long, awkward silence.

"My mother and I . . . we're visiting the beach," said Noah. He pointed towards the cave mouth as though she might not know what was out there. "We're swimming . . . well, she is. I . . . don't really care for swimming. Why don't you . . . come out and join us?"

The cowled head moved from side to side. "I cannot come out into the daylight," said Coira. "Not ever."

He chuckled at that. "Why, are you a vampire or something?" he quipped.

He sensed her puzzlement. "What is a . . . vam . . .?"

"Oh, I was only joking! You know, a vampire? Like . . . Count Dracula?"

"I do not know him."

He thought for a moment, that she was turning his own joke back on him, but then he realised that her voice was flat, open. She really didn't have the faintest idea what he was talking about. He glanced around the interior of the cave and spotted a flat-topped boulder a short distance away. He went over to it and sat down, trying to think of the best way to draw her into conversation.

"So..." he murmured. "I'll ask you again. Was it you looking into my bedroom window, last night?"

She stood there, her head down as though pondering the question. "Aye," she said at last, clearly reluctant to return to the subject. "It was."

"And ... may I ask why?"

"Well, I was intrigued. It has been so long since I saw anybody in there. Hardly anyone, really, since the old man ..."

"The old man? Do you mean Mr Crannach?"

"Aye. Not the first Mr Crannach, of course. I am speaking of the old man who threw himself from the cliff."

"Oh, yes, that was him, sure enough. Only ... I thought that was a long time ago. Before the war."

"The war?" Again that bewildered tone. "Which one?"

"Well, *The* War," said Noah. He was starting to feel a little bit exasperated with the girl. "The *World* War? The *Second* World War?"

"I don't think it came here," said Coira.

Now he could hardly contain his laughter. "Of course, it didn't come here! Why would it? But it happened, didn't it? How can you not know about it? It was in the newspapers . . . on the radio . . . everywhere. My father died in it!"

"Oh. I am sorry for your loss. I did not know your father."

That did it. He got up from the rock and paced about a bit. What was going on here, he asked himself? Was it some kind of elaborate prank that his mother had set up? Some way of taking the rise out of him? He doubted that, it really wasn't her style. But then, what was he to make of this strange girl who wouldn't step into the light, who didn't seem to know anything about what was happening out in the world? It was almost as though she . . .

He stopped pacing. He turned to look at her again.

"Coira?" he said.

"Yes?"

"Do you know how long you've been here? In the cave, I mean."

"Well, ever since my father and I left the hospital."

"Which hospital?"

Now she was pointing towards the cave mouth and once again, he noted that there was something wrong with her hand. There didn't seem to be as many fingers on it as there ought to be.

"The one on the cliff top," she said. "After my mother died, and so many others were sick, my father came to me and said that if we stayed in there, we would be dead mutton too. So we left, and came here."

Noah took a deep breath. "Are you . . . you're not talking about . . . the old leper hospital?" he murmured.

She nodded. "Aye," she said. "It had a name, back then, of course, but I forget what it was."

"But that . . . that's not . . . you can't be . . ." Noah shook his head, not wanting to believe what his mind was telling him. "Mr Morrison said that was in the fifteen hun . . ." His voice gave out and suddenly a panic took him, welling up within him like a balloon that seemed to suddenly burst in his chest, snatching the breath right out of him. Before he quite knew what he was doing, he had turned on his heel and was striding towards the cave mouth, needing the reassurance of the sun on his face.

"Where are you going?" he heard her call, but he ignored her. He got outside and scrambled a short distance down the slope, before he remembered to take a breath. He glanced back towards the cave mouth and saw only darkness within. He registered that he was holding something and looking down, he saw that he still had the conch gripped in his right hand. His first impulse was to fling it aside, as far as he could throw it, but something made him hesitate and then push it back into his jacket pocket.

He carried on walking down the slope, stumbling on the uneven rocks until he got to the beach, only to discover that Millicent was already splashing about happily in the shallows. She noticed him and lifted a hand to wave. He waved back without thinking about it and dropped down into the sand. He sat there staring out to sea, his mind reeling with the only realisation that he could possibly arrive at. He had been talking to a ghost. He didn't know what to think about that, but for the moment at least, he knew he didn't want to go back into that cave. Not until he had things in perspective.

Millicent stood up in the shallows and came striding up the beach, raining drops of water onto the sand. She stopped a short distance away from him and gave him a quizzical look.

"You took your time," she said. "Everything all right?"

He nodded. He stuck an index finger into the sand and traced an abstract pattern into it.

"Well, are you coming in for a splash around?"

He shook his head. "I forgot my swimming togs," he said.

"But . . . I thought . . . didn't you just go back for them?

"I did. Yes. But I . . . changed my mind."

Millicent let out a long sigh of exasperation. "Well, suit yourself," she concluded. "But you're missing out. The water's lovely."

And with that she turned and strolled back to the sea, leaving him to sit alone and ponder.

Chapter Ten

Visitation

H E LAY IN BED, WAITING, HIS GAZE FIXED TO THE blanket that he had draped over the window of his room.

The long afternoon had passed as slowly – as Millicent was so fond of saying – as molasses in winter. After the beach, the two of them had started for home and of course, as they'd picked their way up the steep slope, Millicent had finally noticed the dark opening of the cave.

"Look at that!" she'd exclaimed eagerly, but Noah didn't really want to look. He kept his eyes fixed resolutely on the way ahead as she trilled on about what a simply wonderful setting it would make for her new book and how it would be the perfect hideout for the Adventurers when they were fleeing from . . . whichever bad people she decided to put in the story. There were always bad people in her stories and, of course, the Adventurers always got the better of them. Millicent even announced that she must return to the cave at some point in the near future so she could have "a proper mooch around inside it" – but for now, her first mission was to get back to the cabin to make a proper start on that pesky typescript, because she thought now, that she finally knew how the story would begin . . .

Once back at the cabin, Noah had muttered something about going to his room to read, and had left her sitting at the table, a towel wrapped around her wet hair, staring intently at her typewriter; but reading was really the last thing on Noah's mind. He wanted to try and piece together exactly what had happened to him in the cave. He wanted to come up with a rational explanation for the girl who called herself Coira – one that didn't involve her being in a leper hospital in the sixteenth century. But, try as he might, he couldn't think of anything other than the unnerving fact that he'd recently had a conversation with a dead person.

But that was stupid, he reasoned! Ghosts didn't exist. Everybody knew that. They were just figments of the imagination, silly stories that people used to scare each other . . . except he knew what he'd seen and heard . . . and he really couldn't think of another explanation. Unless the girl was some local, trying to play a trick on him? Except that everybody had told him, there was only one other person living on the island, Mr Finlay, and there was no possible way it could have been him, lurking in the shadows and affecting a young girl's voice . . .

Over a terrible dinner of tinned Irish stew and already stale bread, Millicent had told Noah, grumpily, that she hadn't had a very productive afternoon. The heap of crumpled up sheets of typing paper, which she'd used to light the stove, was testament to that. The great idea she thought she'd had back at the beach simply hadn't worked out.

"I can't seem to get an angle on the story," she told him. "At least, not one I haven't tried a hundred times before."

"Write one about a boy who meets a ghost," suggested Noah, mournfully, spooning another dollop of tasteless stew into his mouth. "That's something you haven't tried."

She gave him a disapproving look. "It's not the kind of thing I write," she told him. "You know I don't go in for all of that supernatural claptrap."

He felt like telling her that neither had *he* until very recently, but decided not to go down that route.

He'd put off going to bed for as long as possible that night, but when Millicent announced that she was turning in, he knew that there was nothing for it but to follow her example. "I thought you said you'd fix up some kind of curtain for my room," he grumbled, and she told him she'd get around to it as soon as she could, and with that, she bid him good night. So, once alone in his room, he took one of the blankets they'd brought with them off his bed and draped it over the window frame telling himself he'd rather be cold than have somebody staring in at him in the middle of the night. With that, he climbed into bed, but he kept a candle burning in its tin holder, a short distance away, despite the fact that Millicent had expressly forbidden him to do so.

"A fire risk," she'd told him, but he didn't care. He only knew that he was afraid of the dark and of what might be lurking in it. He lay on his back for a very long time, staring at the hanging blanket, trying with all his might to stay awake, but as the hours stretched out, his eyes grew heavy and sleep finally placed its powerful grip around him. He sank into the treacly depths where the dream was waiting for him.

It was not the usual sea voyage dream. This was something entirely new and even more unpleasant.

He was up on the cliff top path and it was night time. A full moon hung serenely in a strangely starless sky, gazing benignly down at him, wisps of cloud drifting across its placid face. Noah stood at the top of the steep descent, gazing down at the little cove far below him, which looked quite different in the moonlight. He wasn't sure how he had got here or what had lured him from his bed, but he realised that his feet were bare, he could feel the rough ground beneath the soles of his feet. Something made him reach into the pocket of his jacket and his hand emerged holding the conch. It glittered meaningfully in the light of the moon, as though urging him to play a tune on it. He didn't really want to do that, afraid of what the consequences might be, but somehow, he couldn't help himself.

He lifted the shell to his lips, intending to play *Three Blind Mice*, but when he blew into it, moving his fingers rhythmically up and down, what actually emerged was a tune he had never heard before, a wild, shrill melody that scampered up and down the scale, the notes echoing eerily on the night air. He didn't really like what he was playing, he very much wanted to stop but somehow couldn't bring himself to tear the conch away from his mouth. As he played, he stared down at the sand, which despite the distance, he could see in perfect detail – and as he watched, horrified, something broke through the surface of the sand – a long, bare, wizened arm.

An instant later a second one emerged a short distance from the first and then, from between the limbs, a hideous bony skull. A figure was clambering out from under the sand, not a skeleton exactly, but a long, emaciated manikin, clad in a ragged cloak. As Noah watched, spellbound, the figure began to dance to the tune the conch was making, performing a lurching, shambling jig, those skinny arms upraised to the sky, bare boned fingers gesticulating at the moon. Now another figure was pushing its way up through the sand, this one female, Noah decided, with long coils of ratty blonde hair framing her wasted features. She wore the rotting remains of what must once have been a fine gown, but now was little more than filthy tatters. As Noah continued to play, she moved to stand before the first figure. She performed an eerie curtsy, he gave an elaborate bow and then the two of them danced together, throwing back their heads and laughing, their teeth flashing in the moonlight.

Noah was aware of a thick sweat breaking on his brow, but he could not stop playing, much as he wanted to and as he stared down, wide-eyed in horror, more figures began to push their way up from under the sand – another gangling man wearing the remains of a broad-brimmed hat: a second woman with a canvas bag thrown over a white-boned shoulder: another man! Another woman! Before Noah knew what was happening, the beach was full of dancing couples, twirling and swaying together in an obscene parody of a dance, each of them responding eagerly to the tune that Noah was playing.

Finally, he managed to wrench the conch away from his lips, cutting off the music in mid flow. The creatures stopped in their tracks. As one, they turned their heads to look accusingly up at him and he was uncomfortably aware of the power of their combined gaze boring into him. There was a long silence – perhaps the deepest, most terrifying silence he had ever known. Then one of the creatures threw back his head and howled like a wolf. And as one, the dancers started towards him, scrambling up the steep incline that led to the place where he stood, their mouths open, their arms outstretched to tear at him.

Which was when he realised that his feet were rooted to the spot and that he couldn't move a muscle . . .

He woke with a gasp of terror and was profoundly grateful to realise that he was back in the little bedroom. It was darker than he expected, and he realised that the candle must have burned out, but he was grateful to be where he was, where the hideous dancers could not reach him. He lay on his back, allowing his breathing to return to normal, while his vision became gradually accustomed to the gloom.

His relief was very short-lived. In the half-light, he could just make out a figure standing at the window, its back turned to Noah. It was reaching up its arms to pull down the blanket that Noah had placed there. Noah opened his mouth to ask Millicent what she thought she was doing, but the words died in his throat as he realised that this wasn't Millicent. The blanket fell silently to the ground, allowing in the moonlight, and he saw that the figure was that of a man, a big heavy-set fellow with a thatch of unruly white hair that stuck up from his scalp in tufts. He wore a thick tweed shirt and dark trousers that were held up with braces and he stood there, unmoving, as he stared out into the night as though watching for something.

"Who . . . who are you?" whispered Noah.

The man flinched and turned slowly around to look towards the sound of the voice. Noah stared in mute horror at the pale haggard features that gazed in his direction, without seeming to register him. The man's eyes were cold, expressionless, vacant. They were the eyes of a dead man.

Noah opened his mouth to scream, but he couldn't seem to make a sound, other than a slow exhalation of air. The man continued to stare towards him, his mouth hanging open, as though bewildered. Then he turned abruptly to his right and started towards the closed bedroom door. As Noah watched in stunned disbelief, the man walked right through it.

It was only then that Noah found his voice and let out a yell that he thought, was surely loud enough to wake the dead.

Chapter Eleven

The Hut

"FOR GOODNESS SAKE, NOAH, IT WAS QUITE obviously a dream!"

Millicent sat at the pine table, her arms crossed, her expression suggesting that she would entertain no other explanation. If Noah had thought that she'd be singing a different tune after the long conversation they'd had the previous night, he was to be disappointed. She was adamant that she wasn't going to leave Inchtinn until she was good and ready.

"It wasn't a dream," he insisted. "I've already told you."

"But you cannot seriously expect me to believe the nonsense

you told me last night," she cried. "Dead people dancing a jig in the cove . . ."

"No, that bit *was* a dream! I knew you weren't listening to me. I woke up from that and there was this old man standing in my room. He . . . he took down the blanket I'd hung over the window!"

"We've all had that experience," reasoned Millicent. "You only *think* you've woken up. But really, it's a continuation of the same dream."

Noah shook his head. "That's easy for you to say," he told her. "You weren't there. You didn't see what I saw."

Millicent let out a long sigh. "You know who I blame for this?" she muttered.

Noah looked at her, baffled. "Who?" he asked.

"John bloody Wyndham," she said.

He glared at her. "What's it got to do with him?"

"I told you no good would come of reading that horrible story," she said. "It's quite clearly turned your mind."

"This has nothing to do with *Day of the Triffids*! He doesn't write stories like that, anyway. This was a ghost. I . . . I think it must have been Mr Crannach."

"Who?"

"The old man who lived here."

"How do you even know his name?"

"Mr Finlay mentioned him to me. He also said . . ."

"Go on."

"That he threw himself off the cliff . . ."

"He said, what?" Millicent snorted in disbelief. "I've a good mind to have a serious talk with Mr Finlay. Fancy saying that to an impressionable young boy!"

"It's true though, isn't it?"

"I haven't the foggiest idea. Mr Morrison certainly didn't mention anything like that to me." She frowned, gazed at Noah intently. "Look, I know what you're trying to do," she said.

"What do you mean?"

"You made it abundantly clear that you never wanted to come here. And you hated the place at first sight. It's quite obvious that you want to go home, you've done nothing but complain since we arrived – and it's quite apparent that you're prepared to go to any lengths to get your own way."

Noah stared at her. "Are you saying . . . that I'm making it up?" he cried.

Millicent frowned, as though she suspected she might have gone too far. "Noah, here's the situation. It's really very simple. Whether you like it or not, we're here and we have no contact with the outside world until Mr Morrison returns on Saturday morning. So there's absolutely nothing I can do until then."

"But . . . Mr Finlay has a short wave radio, doesn't he? Mr Morrison said that we could give him a call on that and he'd be over here within the hour."

Millicent actually laughed at that. "If you think I'm going to call him with some hare-brained story about the island being haunted, you've got another thing coming," she told him. "He'll think I've gone insane." She pushed back her chair and stood up. "Now, if you've quite finished prattling on, I'd like to get some breakfast sorted, so I can get on with my writing."

"But you're not even doing any," snapped Noah, feeling suddenly vindictive. "You're just tapping out a few words, and then crumpling up the paper. Anybody could do that. *I* could do that! Perhaps it's time you admitted that you haven't got it in you to be a writer anymore."

Millicent looked outraged. "What nonsense! Of course I have it in me! I'm just having a few hiccups, that's all . . ."

"You've been having hiccups ever since Father died," said Noah, relishing the way she winced when he said the words. "And, anyway, I don't understand why it's so important to you. It's not as if you need the money, is it?"

"It was never about the money!" cried Millicent. "It was about being a *writer*. That's the one thing I have since Archie left us and I won't let anything take it away from me." She glared at Noah. "Not even you."

They stood there glaring at each other in angry silence for a moment. Then Noah got up from his seat and strode towards the door.

"Where are you going?" Millicent asked him, fearfully.

"Sit back down and I'll make you some breakfast."

"I'm not hungry," he said, not even bothering to look back at her over his shoulder. "I'm going out."

"Where are you going?" she called after him.

"*Out*," he snapped back. "You stay here and write your precious book. You obviously care a lot more about that than you do about me!"

He threw the door open, stepped outside and slammed it behind him. Then he started walking and he didn't look back.

He went around the cabin to the back garden and started along the track that led up to the cliffs. He'd only gone a short distance when he heard Millicent calling out his name, but he ignored her and kept walking. When he finally did look over his shoulder, he saw that she had given up and gone back inside. Good enough for her, he thought. It was time she realised that there were more important things in the world than her ridiculous children's stories. Something needed to be done about what had happened last night and it looked as though he was the only one prepared to make the effort. Right then...

Pretty soon, the track was rising steeply through the crags and the birds were in their usual positions, fluttering their wings and letting out indignant squawks as he went by, but he put his head down and kept walking, even when a couple of birds flapped noisily past him only a few feet above his unprotected head. He kept up his pace and had soon left them behind. When he reached the top of the ridge, he paused for a while to glance to his left at the cave mouth and he considered going back in there, but decided he wasn't ready for that. Right now, his priority was to contact Mr Morrison; so he angled left and followed the undulating path along the ridge. Grey crags towered above him on the left of the track and after he had walked for about twenty minutes, he noticed another path leading steeply up into the rocks and he saw the tops of some ruined buildings up there. This must be the old leper hospital that both Coira and Mr Finlay had mentioned, he decided, ugly grey buildings that seemed to sprout up out of the basalt like some kind of organic thing, growing from the rock. Once again, Noah thought about heading up there to explore them, but decided that right now he would do better to keep to his original intention.

He walked onwards and after another fifteen minutes or so, the track began to descend as it neared the far side of the island. Sure enough, he saw that he was approaching a wooden hut perched on an outcrop to the right of the track, a tiny, dilapidated affair, much smaller than the cabin Noah and Millicent were staying in. There was no sign of life outside, but a plume of grey smoke was rising from a metal chimney that jutted up from the apex of the roof. Noah approached the door and reached up his knuckles to tap politely on the weathered wood. There was a long silence, before a muffled voice from within said, "Enter."

Noah turned the handle, pushed the door open and peered cautiously inside. The interior of the hut was uncomfortably hot, Noah thought, mostly because a little pot-bellied stove was blazing in one corner. Mr Finlay was sitting at a large table that was piled high with all manner of things: books, jars, a pair of binoculars, glass cases, dirty dishes and, Noah noticed, a glass that was half-full of an amber liquid. Mr Finlay wore a grubby vest, the sleeves of which were rolled up to his elbows and he was appraising Noah with interest, an unpleasant smile on his bearded face. There were tiny beads of sweat on his forehead. "Well, well, you didn't hang around, did you?" he observed. He looked towards the open door as if expecting somebody else. "Your famous mother not with you?" he added.

"Er . . . no, she's . . . writing."

"Of course she is! Far too grand to grace my humble abode with her presence, I'm sure. Well, come along in if you're coming and close that door behind you. You're letting all the heat out."

Noah did as he was told, wondering why Mr Finlay needed it to be quite so hot on what was, after all, a bright sunny morning – but by way of explanation, the ornithologist waved a hand at a rectangular glass case on the table, which contained several small, speckled eggs, nestled on straw. "This clutch was abandoned by the mother," he said. "I'm trying to get them to hatch out. So, naturally, I need it to be hot in here."

"I see." Noah edged closer to the table and took a closer look. "What kind of bird do they belong to?" he asked.

"Guillemots," said Mr Finlay.

"Oh yes, you said they were the fierce ones, didn't you?"

"Well-remembered." Mr Finlay lifted the glass from the table and took a generous gulp from its contents. Close up, Noah thought, he smelled quite strongly of alcohol and there was a thick, slurred quality to his voice that suggested that he might have already drunk quite a few glasses, despite it still being early morning. "I'm expecting this batch to pop at any moment, but that bit's relatively easy. Persuading the parents to accept the chicks afterwards, that's the tricky part. It needs to be done in the early hours of the morning." He studied Noah, seemingly amused by the boy's presence. "So," he said. "What can I do for you?"

Noah swallowed. "Mr Morrison told me you have a radio," he said.

"Did he, now? Why, were you hoping to catch *Educating Archie*? Or perhaps you're a fan of the *Billy Cotton Band Show*?"

Noah shook his head. He was convinced that Mr Finlay had purposely misunderstood his request, just for his own amusement.

"No, I meant . . . a short wave radio. I was hoping perhaps you might be able to call Mr Morrison for me?"

Mr Finlay chuckled. "And what would you want with that old rascal?" he murmured. "Is there a problem? Accommodation not living up to expectation?"

Noah stared at the man, suspiciously. "You know something, don't you?" he said. "About the cabin?"

Mr Finlay shrugged his shoulders. "I know that the few people who've ventured to sleep there since old man Crannach breathed his last haven't chosen to stay for very long." He chuckled unpleasantly, took another gulp of his drink. "Let me hazard a guess," he said. "I reckon you've seen somebody in there. An old man with white hair."

"Yes!" Noah felt briefly elated and then annoyed. "You . . . knew about it?" he cried. "And you didn't say anything?"

Mr Finlay affected an innocent look. "What would I have said? You'd probably have thought I'd spent too long out here on my own. Something I've been suspecting, anyway, for quite some time. And besides, who was to say you'd see the same thing that the others saw? Let me assure you, I've never clapped eyes on this . . . *apparition* that people talk about. I only have their word for it." He chuckled. "The last chap who stayed there was very agitated. A hill walker, he was. Couldn't wait to head back to the mainland. Luckily for him, he had his own boat, so he was able to sail away. Mind you, he did make a bit of a discovery while he was there . . ."

"Oh, what was that?"

Mr Finlay looked thoughtful for a moment. "Now let me think, where did I put it? Oh yes . . ." He got up from the table and padded over to an old chest of drawers. Noah saw that he was barefoot and that his feet were absolutely plastered with ingrained dirt. He crouched down, pulled open a drawer and took out a tattered notebook. He brought it back to the table and handed it to Noah. "There you go," he said. "I take it you *do* read?"

"Of course. But what is it?"

"It's the diary of old man Crannach," said Mr Finlay, with a grin. "The hill walker told me he found it hidden under some floorboards in one of the bedrooms." He waggled his eyebrows. "Didn't say what else he was looking for under there. Probably hoped the old man had left a few treasures hidden away. Instead, he found that and thought he'd pass it on to my safe keeping."

Noah frowned. "Have you read it?" he asked.

"Bits of it. He's not much of a writer, to tell you the truth. Not in your Mother's league, I'm sure. But it explains a lot." He gave Noah a sly wink. "Bit of bedtime reading for you, since you're so interested."

"Thank you. I'll make sure you get it back before we leave." Noah took the notebook and found that it fit perfectly into his jacket pocket. He thought for a moment. "Did . . . did Mr Morrison know about all this?" he asked. "The ghost?" It had occurred to him that the old man had said quite a few things about how strange Inchtinn was, but he'd never mentioned that the cabin was haunted.

"I honestly have no idea," said Mr Finlay. "I've certainly never spoken to him about it and he's never mentioned it to me. But then, he hasn't really spent any time on the island since Crannach died, so . . . he probably wouldn't have a clue. Morrison is a bit of an old rapscallion, but I don't believe there's any harm in him." He studied Noah thoughtfully. "The thing is . . . what are you going to do?"

Noah looked at him for a moment. "The radio?" he murmured.

"Ah yes. It's over there."

Mr Finlay pointed to a wide wooden shelf beside a window. Spread out on it was a haphazard collection of components – Bakelite shapes, wires, what looked to Noah like a heap of fuses and valves. He stepped over to the shelf and picked up a piece of oddly shaped metal, turned it around in his fingers. "How am I supposed to make a call on this?" he asked.

Mr Finlay chuckled. "A very good question – and one I've been asking myself for the last couple of days. The damned thing's gone kaput, I'm afraid. I've taken it apart and put it back together again three times now and can I get it to work?" He shook his head. "No I cannot. So I suppose my only option is to wait until the RSPB supply boat gets here to see if they've got anything that can sort out the problem."

Noah turned back to look at him. "And when is that due?" he asked hopefully.

"In a month's time."

Noah's heart sank. "But . . . Mr Morrison will be here in one week," he said.

"Ah, well, there you are then! That will solve both our problems. Perhaps you'd be kind enough to ask him to drop by here and I'll get him to visit my employers on the mainland and inform them about the radio . . ."

"But . . . what are we to do until then?" cried Noah. "We can't stay in a place that's haunted!"

Mr Finlay nodded. "I take your point," he said. "But what are your alternatives? Obviously, I can't invite you to stay here, there's hardly room to swing the proverbial cat." He seemed to ponder for a moment. "If it's any consolation, I've never heard of anybody being hurt in the cabin. My understanding is that the old man is agitated but harmless. One of the chaps who'd seen him claimed that he appeared to be looking for something . . ."

"He didn't seem harmless to me," retorted Noah. "He was . . . terrifying."

"Hmm. I expect so. What does your mother think about it?"

"She hasn't seen him. She seems to think I've made the whole thing up."

Mr Finlay smiled. "I thought writers were supposed to be

the ones with vivid imaginations," he said.

"I didn't imagine it," insisted Noah.

"No, I wasn't saying that." Mr Finlay picked up his glass of whisky and studied the contents as though he thought he might find an answer there. "I'm told these things are quite spectacular when they happen . . ."

"I know I don't much fancy spending another night in that place," said Noah gloomily.

"It's summer," mused Mr Finlay. "And we haven't had rain for a while. I suppose you could sleep out in the garden. I don't imagine Mr Crannach ever leaves his precious cabin. Do you have a tent or anything like that?"

Noah shook his head. "Do you?"

Mr Finlay shook his head. "Of course, there are the old hospital buildings . . ."

"I saw those on the way here," murmured Noah. "They didn't look very welcoming."

"No, but don't discount them. They're derelict, of course, but the main building still has a fairly sound roof over most of it. Amazing, considering its age. But of course, they knew how to build in those days . . ." Mr Finlay drained the last of the whisky. "By all accounts, it's the hospital that got old man Crannach all fired up in the first place."

Noah came back to the table and settled into an empty seat opposite the ornithologist. "Whatever do you mean?" he asked.

"You'd need to read the diary," said Mr Finlay. "It's all in there. But it's hard going." He waved a hand dismissively. "As I said, a small time writer, not remotely up to your mother's standard..."

"Oh, so you *have* heard of her then?" observed Noah, sharply. "Why did you pretend you hadn't?"

Mr Finlay shrugged. "Ach, I don't know. It's just my manner, I suppose. If you want to know the truth, I hate to show that I'm impressed by anyone. But of course I've heard of her. She's famous, isn't she?"

"I suppose so," admitted Noah.

"And those are the kind of people we venerate these days. Writers of fanciful stories. People who tell lies for a living. But you try telling them a plain truth and see how quickly they become bored. Tell them about what's happening to the natural world. The way we're decimating our native species ... how in fifty years time we'll have wiped out half of the creatures on the planet. Not so interested then, eh?"

Noah tried not to lose patience with Mr Finlay. "You were telling me about Mr Crannach's book?" he prompted.

Mr Finlay scowled. "Oh, aye. Well, it turns out that old man Crannach was a descendant of the fellow who originally built and ran the leper hospital. The two of them shared the same name. As I understood it, Crannach moved out here when he retired, intending to do some research into the history of the hospital, but when he found out what had actually happened there, well . . . it sort of unhinged him."

"But . . . what *had* happened?"

Mr Finlay waved a hand in dismissal. "It's ages since I read it. Suffice to say that Crannach's glorious ancestor was not quite the hero that he was cracked up to be . . ." Mr Finlay chuckled unpleasantly, then reached under the table and lifted something from the floor – a half-filled bottle of whisky. He topped up his glass and swirled the contents around for a moment, gazing at it woozily. "Ah, there's nothing like a good single malt," he murmured. "It's the one thing that gets me through the days."

Noah looked at him. "Why do the job if you hate it so much?" he asked.

"I don't hate it," Mr Finlay assured him. "Not exactly. It's just that I get a wee bit bored."

Noah gazed down at the scatter of junk on the table top. "How am I going to persuade Millicent that we should move out of the cabin?" he mused. "She won't believe me anyway. She'll just say I'm being *nervous*." He studied Finlay for a moment. "What about the cave?" he asked. "The one that overlooks the beach?"

"I wouldn't think that's a good place to sleep," said Mr Finlay.

"I didn't mean that. It's just that you said something about it the first time we spoke."

"Did I?"

"Yes. You said . . . "Nobody ever goes in there." What did you mean by that?"

Mr Finlay shrugged his narrow shoulders. "Well, I only meant it's dark and the ground's treacherous."

"You've never seen anyone in there? A girl?"

Mr Finlay looked blankly back at him. "No," he said. "Why, have you?"

There was a long silence then, while they stared at each other. Noah got to his feet. "I'd better get going," he said. He pointed to the shelf with the jumble of radio components. "If you should manage to get that thing working, please come and tell me."

"Alright," said Mr Finlay. "But I wouldn't hold your breath. I'm really not that handy when it comes to popular mechanics." He raised his glass in a mock toast. "Cheers," he said. "Sweet dreams."

And with that, Noah turned and went back outside, into the sunshine.

Chapter Twelve

The Hospital

H E HAD FULLY INTENDED TO HEAD STRAIGHT back to the cabin, but when he came to the place where a steep narrow track led up to the hospital ruins, he found himself changing direction and climbing the slope instead. Higher up, it opened up a little and the ground levelled out to reveal the rocky cliff top. Pretty soon, he was approaching the nearest of the buildings, a large oblong construction made from blocks of roughly hewn grey stone. A heavy wooden door hung open on broken hinges. Noah stepped cautiously through the opening and stood for a moment in the spacious interior, looking warily around.

As Mr Finlay had said, there was still a roof on the building, though there were holes in several places that allowed narrow shafts of sunlight to pierce the gloom, and birds flapped frantically around in the rafters, the sound of their wings echoing eerily. Something immediately struck Noah as rather strange. The building didn't appear to have any windows, so most of the interior was cloaked in patches of heavy shadow. One section of a nearby wall, however, was illuminated by a bright beam of sunlight coming in through a gap in the roof and Noah realised that this section of it was covered with words that had been scratched into the stone with sharp objects. He stepped closer to inspect them. They mostly consisted of names and dates – THOMAS, 1543 was one that he noticed, and POWELL 1547, another. When he looked more closely, he saw that every spare inch of the stone had something incised into it, the words crowding against each other and in some cases, actually overlapping. There were strange little pictures too – grinning faces, an amateurish attempt at a horse, a crudely drawn flower. One image was a depiction of a cloaked man wearing an odd-looking bird-shaped mask. The man was carrying a stick and was aiming the point of it at a second man, who was crouched on his knees, his hands covering his face. Underneath the image, a single word has been crudely etched into the stone. *Contagion.*

Noah turned away from the wall and walked further into

the building, his feet crunching on a litter of detritus – straw, driftwood, stones, bits of crumbly white chalk. Looking around, he decided that it might just be possible to lay out a couple of sleeping bags here, but he could imagine Millicent's horrified expression if he brought her here and suggested such an action. The problem was, she hadn't seen what Noah had seen, last night. He was pretty sure that one glimpse of Mr Crannach's ravaged features would be enough to make her change her mind about staying in the cabin any longer. But of course, he hoped it would never come to that – that his terrifying glimpse of the old man's ghost would prove to be a once-only experience.

He remembered the notebook in his pocket and looking around, he spotted a broken wooden cabinet lying on its side. He dragged it into an area where there was a little more light, sat down on it and took out the notebook. He opened it to the first page, which was covered with line after line of neatly written script in faded black ink.

Michael J. Crannach, 1938

Today I moved into the old cabin, left to me in my father's will all those years ago. The builders have carried out my instructions to the letter (though they certainly took their time over the work!) and now it is fully restored and once more habitable.

Since the death of my wife, Isabelle, three years ago, I have decided to devote what is left of my life to discovering as much as I can about my illustrious ancestor, Obediah Crannach. Call it an interest, call it an obsession, call it an unfulfilled yearning, but it has always angered me that this great man appears to have been so totally forgotten by the historians. He was after all, an important philanthropist, a man who devoted his life to caring for the sick and needy – but where is his legacy? Has there ever been a statue raised to him in his hometown of Fife? There has not. Has any writer ever produced a biography of him? No, not so far as I am aware and certainly not for the want of looking! Indeed, my attempts to discover more about him, by researching in Scotland's public libraries has yielded no results whatsoever. It is as though history has forgotten him, as though he has been deliberately erased from collective memory. I feel that living here, on the very island where his greatest achievements were made, will aid me in my quest to uncover more about this great but apparently forgotten man . . .

Noah frowned. Mr Finlay hadn't been exaggerating when he'd said that Mr Crannach's writing was on the dull side. There was a lot more of that kind of stuff to follow. An account of his first day settling in, a mention of his regular trips to the mainland for supplies of food and fuel. Noah skimmed through the pages, pausing only whenever a particular phrase caught his eye . . .

Today I discovered a little sandy cove – a beautiful sanctuary that offers a welcome place to lie in the sun and dream my dreams . . . but who, I wonder, has felt the need to mar its beauty with the bleak message I found carved into the rock? "God have Mercy on us." What could have inspired some poor wretch to chisel those words? And why make them so big, as though they really were a plea for help? I understand that much of Obediah's work was with the mentally ill, but what can have inspired some unknown hand to inscribe such a dismal utterance?

Noah flicked through more pages. Another section caught his eye.

The old hospital building feels so austere, so lonely. I spent hours studying the scores of names scratched into the walls, hoping that perhaps I would see a Crannach listed there, or at least another that meant something to my family history, but there were only the names of countless strangers. What happened to all the patients that lived and died here? Why have I found no record of them anywhere else? They too seem to have vanished into the mists of time . . .

The entries continued, listing the late Mr Crannach's fruitless search for information. He had, it seemed, wandered over every inch of the island looking for clues about his ancestor but had found nothing of any use to him. Impatient, Noah flicked onwards and found another entry that was of particular interest.

Today I explored one of the caves in the cliffs overlooking the beach. It is a huge place, the roof as high as a cathedral. I found evidence in there of human habitation – an old fireplace and some discarded fish bones that seemed to suggest that people had lived there at some point. All the time I searched around by the light of a lantern, I had the strangest feeling that I was being observed – that somebody or something was watching me. I cannot fully explain the sensation I had, nor can I explain the fact that I feel sure that the cave has an important contribution to make to my quest. I intend to return tomorrow to make a more thorough search of the place . . .

There was only one more entry after that and Noah immediately noticed a dramatic change. Where before the handwriting had been neat and precise, now it was jagged and sprawling, specked with drops of ink as though whoever had written the words was doing so in a state of extreme agitation.

Now I know the truth, and it is destroying me!
It turns out that my ancestor was not the plaster saint

I have always imagined him to be. On the contrary, he was a charlatan, a confidence trickster, at best a common thief! The charitable institution he set up was a total sham and he made his money by exploiting the very people he pretended to care about – the helpless, the sick and the dying. It nearly kills me to say it, but Obediah grew rich upon their misery. He took their money, he took their property and upon these shameful pickings, he founded his corrupt empire. Little wonder there is no statue to him! Those who learned the truth about his deeds must have wanted to forget that he ever existed – to expunge his foul deeds from the history books forever!

And to think that I used to proudly boast that he was my relative . . . this beast, this monster!

The worst thing is that I cannot tell anyone how I came by this information – if I did, they would surely think me insane. Suffice to say that a voice of reason has come to me, one that I am convinced has spoken only the truth – and it is a truth that I cannot for the life of me, endure. I feel sick with the knowledge that has been granted to me – sick and horribly ashamed.

The man I idolised has turned out to be an idol with feet of clay. My first impulse now is to hide this book away from sight where nobody will ever find it. I need to think long and hard about what I should do on this matter. Perhaps in the fullness of time, I may come to believe that the world should learn of Obediah Crannach's deceit, even if it means that his memory will be eternally damned. But how can I prove what I have learned?

Because of the strange way in which the knowledge has been granted to me, how can I ever hope to convince anyone that I haven't lost my mind?

There was nothing else in the book – the following pages were blank. Noah sat there, staring at them, thinking about what he'd just read. Mr Crannach had said that "a voice of reason" had come to him – and it wasn't hard to decide who that voice must have belonged to. There really was only one possibility.

Noah froze when he became aware of a soft sound behind him – a slow breath being exhaled – and he realised that he was no longer alone in the ruined building. He turned slowly in his seat, tensing himself ready to make a run for it – but he already knew who it would be.

She was standing in the furthest corner of the room, a place where no shafts of light could reach her and once again, she was dressed in that same shapeless hooded cloak, her hands hidden by her long sleeves. As before, he couldn't see her features but he could feel her eyes burning into him with an intensity that made his skin crawl.

"Hello," he said, awkwardly. He didn't know what else to say, and had to admit that under the circumstances, it was a pretty odd thing to choose. Why, he wondered, wasn't he running for the door, yelling his head off? Why wasn't he screaming? She was a ghost, for goodness sake! She had been dead for hundreds of years!

"Hello," said Coira and her tiny voice somehow managed to fill that single word with an eternity of sorrow.

"I thought..." He frowned, not entirely sure what he wanted to say. "I thought you said ... you couldn't leave the cave?"

The cowled head moved slightly from side to side. "I never said that."

"Er ... I'm pretty sure you did."

"No. I said I couldn't step out into the daylight. But here in the shadows is a place I can be. The light cannot touch me here."

"But ... Coira, I don't understand. Wouldn't you need to walk around in the daylight in order to *get* here?"

A short pause. "I do not travel on foot," she said, as if that explained everything.

"Well, then, how ...?"

"I thought you might have come back to the cave," she interrupted him. "I thought after our first talk, you might want to speak to me again."

"I ..."

"After I took such trouble to talk to you, I thought you might be interested to know more. But you did not return."

There was definitely a note of accusation in her voice. "Perhaps you were too busy."

"Well . . ." he said. "I . . . I hadn't really decided what to do about it. I was . . . a little confused, to tell you the truth. I . . . I've never met anybody like you before. And to be honest, I wasn't sure if you were real or if maybe I'd gone a little bit . . . you know, crazy."

"And what do you think now?"

"I'm starting to think that maybe Millicent was right about John Wyndham."

"Who is . . . John . . .?"

"Never mind." Noah looked around, trying to come up with a way to make some rational conversation with her. "So, why did you follow me here?" he asked, waving a hand at his surroundings.

She gave a long sigh. "Because I wanted to tell you more about this place. I was a patient here."

Noah shook his head. "Now, you see, you said that to me before, didn't you? And, I hear what you're saying, but . . . well, it can't be true."

"Why not?" She sounded offended now.

"Well, mostly because Mr Morrison told me it was a hospital in the 1500s. That's . . . that's 400 years ago?"

"Yes?"

"400 years! Well, you're not seriously trying to tell

me that you've been hanging around for all that time. Are you?"

She made no attempt to answer that question. "I was a patient here," she repeated tonelessly. "Me and my parents."

Chapter Thirteen

Contagion

NOAH STARED ACROSS THE ROOM AT HER. "YOU and your parents," he repeated quietly. "I see. And you were . . ." He hesitated to use the word. "You were lepers?"

"There was a contagion," said Coira. "We never gave it any other name. But it could come to people without warning and if you showed the signs of it, then you knew instantly what would happen if others found out. My mother was the first to be stricken."

"Your mother?"

"Aye. It was at our family home in Fife. She found lesions

on her shoulder, and she kept them hidden from our servants and neighbours, but then one appeared on her face. At first, she was able to mask it with powder but it soon got worse and she could hide it no longer."

"I see..."

"I suppose somebody must have informed on us. Neighbours, probably, afraid that the contagion would spread to them and lay them low. At any rate, uniformed men came and knocked on the door of our house one morning, banging upon the oak as though they intended to smash it down. We were told we would all have to leave, with whatever we could carry."

Noah stared at her. "What, just like that?"

"Aye. They didn't waste any time. The idea was to halt the spread of the illness. A coach took us directly to the docks and a boat carried us out to this island. The people that took us kept their faces covered under cloth masks. My father was a wealthy man, and he pleaded that if we could be spared our fate he would reward the men handsomely, but they paid him no heed. We had to leave everything behind. Everything we owned."

"That doesn't seem fair," said Noah, realising even as he said it, what a crashing understatement it was. "I mean... didn't you have anyone who could help you? Friends... family..."

"Our friends did not want to know us, because they would have had to admit that they had been in our company and might have been exposed to the contagion. And then they would be in the same boat as us. Our family, such as they were, could do nothing to help. I don't know what happened to our house. All the lovely things my parents owned . . . the fine furniture, the oil paintings, the souvenirs my father had collected on his travels around the world . . . all were taken from us. We learned later that everything was sold. The money was supposed to pay for our welfare but of course, we never saw any of it. We learned in time where that money had gone. Stolen."

Noah shook his head, trying to imagine what it would be like to be dispossessed, to lose everything you owned. But it was hard for a boy who had always had pretty much whatever he wanted to picture anything like that.

"But," he ventured. "They . . . looked after you in the hospital, yes?"

Again, that slow shake of the head. "They called it a hospital but it was not deserving of the name." Her voice was loaded with contempt now. "It was a charnel house, run by a man called Doctor Obediah Crannach."

Noah sighed and lifted the exercise book. "Yes, I was just reading about him," he said. "This was written by the other Mr Crannach, the one who lived in the cabin where my mother and I are staying. The man who . . . died. He says that he found something out about his ancestor. I suppose . . . I suppose it must have been you that told him the truth."

Coira didn't answer that.

"So what had this Obediah Crannach done that was so wrong?"

"He was one of the wealthiest men in Scotland. He presented himself to the world as a good man, a saintly man, but in truth he was a cruel and greedy exploiter of human misery. He only visited the island once a month to oversee the running of the hospital and when he came, he wore a leather mask filled with dried flowers, so that the contagion would not reach him. We never saw his face, but people told us he lived in luxury in a big house on the mainland and that he dined on the finest meat and drank the most expensive wine. Some said he wasn't a real doctor at all, that he had no medical training."

"*Who* said?"

"The other patients."

"Oh, so there were more of you?"

"We were legion. There were scores of us, all packed into this building." She lifted her head to gaze around the room as if picturing it. "There were rows of beds then, lining the walls," she said. "A curtain ran across the middle of the room to separate the men from the women, but really, we all slept together, side-by-side, cheek by jowl. If they ran out of beds, which they often did, some patients would be made to lie upon the floor. Everyone there had some kind of contagion. Plague . . . smallpox . . . cholera . . . there were other names that I cannot remember. The room stank of corruption. Food and medicine was supposedly sent over to the island every few days from the mainland, by friends and relatives of the sick . . . but we never saw any of it. Doctor Crannach took it for himself and sold it on to others, that's what some patients said. We had only slops to eat and no real medicine to ease our pains, while he led a life of luxury. When people died . . . and so many of us did . . . the bodies were carried away and burned on a bonfire out on the cliff top."

Noah listened, horrified. He was thinking about the words he had just read – how the awful truth had made the other Mr Crannach lose his mind.

"Couldn't anybody *do* something?" he gasped. "To stop it?"

"We were beyond help," murmured Coira. "We were the infected, the damned. Nobody ever came near us."

"But . . . there must have been . . . nurses, surely?"

"There were only *foul clengers*."

"I'm sorry, what are foul . . .?"

"They were men who had suffered from plague themselves, but somehow recovered. They were thought to be safe from infection, but still they covered their faces with leather masks whenever they came into the room. They brought us our food, such as it was and they dragged out the bodies of those who had died, so they could be burned."

Noah didn't know what to say now. He was simply horrified. Coira kept talking as though she desperately needed to unburden herself of the memories.

"My mother didn't last more than a few days," she said, her voice trembling with emotion. "I held her as she died and told her I would always keep her memory alive – then she gave a kind of shudder and a last breath and went limp in my arms. They carried her away. My father asked if we might be allowed to leave after that, but they said, no, we could be infected ourselves. My father pleaded with them, but they would not heed his words. And then, I started showing signs of the contagion myself and my father came to me and whispered that we had to get out of there at any cost or we would both surely meet the same fate as Mother."

"So . . . what did you do?"

Coira's voice was quieter now as if even after all this time, she was afraid of being overheard. "When we were first taken from our home, my father hid something about his person – a diamond. It was a family heirloom and worth a lot of money. He still had the diamond hidden safely away, so he talked secretly to one of the *foul clengers*, a man called Jake and promised him the diamond if he would help us to escape."

"And this Jake agreed to help you?"

"Not at first. He was scared of what might happen to him if he was found out, and told us he had two young children back on the mainland who depended on his pay. My father told him the money he'd get for the diamond would keep his children in food for a very long time and he finally agreed to it and even enlisted another man to aid him. The next time bodies were taken out to be burned, Jake and his friend arranged to have the two of us carried away on stretchers, covered by blankets. We had to lie very still and make no sound, even when we were prodded with sticks as we were carried out. We were taken up to the cliffs with the dead." She sighed. "The feeling when the blanket was pulled back and I found myself gazing up into the blue sky . . . it was the best feeling in the world. It was magical."

Noah nodded. "What happened next?" he asked.

"My father gave Jake his diamond. That was the moment when he could have betrayed us. He could have taken his prize and dragged us back to the hospital . . . but he was a man of his word. He allowed us to leave. But he warned us that if anybody caught us and asked how we had escaped, he would deny all knowledge of us. We were on our own. That's when we found the cave and made it our home." She sighed. "We had to be careful," she said. "If anybody from the hospital had seen us, other than the ones who had helped, we knew that we would be dragged back in chains."

"So . . . how did you survive?"

"It wasn't easy. Jake had given my father a fishing line and some hooks and we would fish from the beach whenever we could and cook whatever we caught over a fire made of driftwood. Sometimes, when supplies were dropped at the jetty – the things that were supposed to have been for us anyway –

we could manage to creep up and steal a few small morsels for ourselves. But, the contagion was already upon me. I was growing weaker by the day and my father could see that. He must have been going out of his mind with worry. The situation became desperate. So he told me that he had made up his mind – he was going to go for help to the mainland. He said he would find a boat over there and sail it back himself if he had to . . ."

"But . . . how was he going to get to the mainland?"

Another long sigh. "He told me he would swim."

"Swim?" Noah thought about the island as he had first seen it from the jetty on the far side of the firth – that tiny, distant grey smudge on the horizon. The image made his stomach lurch. "Is that even possible?" he gasped.

"My father believed so. He was always a very strong swimmer, you see. He had found a big piece of driftwood that he said he would use as a float. He told me to settle myself in the cave and to wait for his return. He promised me that however long it took, he would come back for me and that he would take me to the mainland. Once there, we would find somebody who would help us. Then he left and went down to the beach. I stood in the cave mouth and watched him prepare himself. I watched him swim away. I watched until he was out of sight. Then I settled down to wait for him. I waited and waited. I'm still waiting . . ."

Noah stared at her in disbelief. "Oh, but you surely can't

think . . . you don't think he might still come back? He must be . . ."

"What?" she asked him.

He'd been about to say that her father must be dead, but at the last moment, it had occurred to him that Coira must be dead, too. And she was still here, wasn't she? She was standing right there talking to him! But was he honestly supposed to believe that she been haunting this island for over 400 years? That she had spent all that time alone in the cave, gazing out to the horizon and waiting for a rescue that would never come? He felt suddenly light-headed. He dropped the notebook, put his head in his hands and took a couple of deep breaths.

"Are you all right?" asked Coira, moving a little closer.

"I'm trying to get it straight," he told her. "I just need a moment to . . . think about this."

"As you wish," she said.

He sat there, trying to order the jumble of confused thoughts that were crashing around in his head and then homed in on the thing that was most pressing to him. "All right, so . . . it's obvious that you spoke to Mr Crannach . . . that you told him everything that had happened to you."

"Aye," murmured Coira. "The old man. He came to the cave looking for answers. I could sense that he needed to know the truth. It was all he cared about. So I spoke to him. I told him my story."

"I've seen him," said Noah. "Last night. He was in my room, staring out of the window. That was . . . pretty scary."

"You are right to be scared," she assured him. "His is a restless spirit. He is full of anger over what his ancestor did. It was that knowledge that made him take his own life."

"Why did you tell him?"

"Because I felt sorry for him. And . . . I needed to talk to someone. I hadn't spoken a word to a living person since my father left. And . . . he was searching for information about the hospital, you see and I knew I could give him that, but . . . I didn't realise the effect my words would have on him. I didn't know that they would fill him with shame and anger. He had always thought his ancestor was a noble man, a kindly man . . . he told me that he had always believed that Obediah deserved to be feted by society, that he should have been awarded medals for his charity . . . and to be told that he was a cruel exploiter of the sick was the last thing he wanted to hear! I should have realised that. I should have spared him the knowledge, but it had been so long since I had spoken to anyone that I didn't even pause to think of the consequences. I was trying to help! I told him everything. After I had finished talking, he went back to the cabin and drank a whole bottle of whisky. I tried to speak to him again, but he would not heed me. He was a broken man. Then, late one night, after another long drinking session, something must have overtaken him. He ran up to the cliffs and . . ."

"I know what he did," said Noah, hastily. For some reason, he didn't want to picture the old man tumbling to his death onto the rocks below. "I know all about it," he said again, just in case there might be any doubt. "But the thing is, Coira, me and my mother, we're staying in his cabin . . . and I'm afraid he might hurt us."

"You are right to be afraid," said Coira. "He hates anybody being in his home. He died angry, you see, angry at the world and what could be allowed to happen in it. I tried to warn you not to go there."

"Did you?" Noah was puzzled. "I don't remember . . ."

"You need to go back and tell your mother that the two of you have to leave. Today, before darkness comes again. That's when he is most powerful."

"But . . ." Noah shook his head. "She won't listen to me. She never listens!"

"Then you must make her listen! Do you understand?" She reached out a hand towards him and for a moment, the sleeve of her cloak lifted and he caught a glimpse of that hand. He stared at it. He didn't want to stare, but somehow couldn't help himself. It was a twisted grey claw, with only one finger and a thumb remaining. She seemed to sense his discomfort, because she quickly concealed the hand back in the folds of fabric.

"I'm sorry," he said. "I didn't mean to stare. I . . ." He floundered for something to say. "Does it . . . hurt?"

Again that long sigh. "Not any more," she said.

He got up from the box he was sitting on and took a few steps towards her but she shrank away from him, as though reluctant to let him come closer. "Won't you let me see your face?" he murmured.

The cowled head shook. "No. I am not ... fit to be looked at."

"I just ... it's hard to talk to somebody you can't see," he told her.

"Trust me," she said. "You do not want to see my face."

"But ..."

"You should go now," she said. "You need to talk to your mother. You need to persuade her to leave the cabin. Before it's too late."

"Can Mr Crannach hurt us, then? I thought gh ..." He felt strangely awkward using the word in front of her. "I thought ghosts were just ... sounds and noises."

"Is that how I appear to you? Harmless?" She seemed to think for a moment and then she turned her head slightly to look at the wooden box that he had just been sitting on. Noah turned his head to follow her gaze, just in time to see the heavy box lurch suddenly upwards from the ground and go tumbling through the air to smash against the nearest wall with a loud crash. Noah's heart seemed to leap in his chest. He stared at the splintered pile of wood that lay scattered on the floor, then turned back towards Coira. "How did you ...?"

But she was gone. The dark corner of the room where she had been standing a moment earlier was now completely empty. Noah said something under his breath, something that Millicent, had she been present, would definitely not have approved of.

Then he turned and hurried back to the doorway. He stepped outside and stood for a moment, blinking in the bright sunlight, his thoughts twisting and turning like a nest of serpents in his head. What was he to make of what had just happened? Had he really been talking to the ghost of a leper, or like Mr Crannach before him, had he simply lost his mind? He really didn't know what to think on that score but of one thing, he was certain.

He needed to persuade Millicent that they should get out of the cabin before it was too late. And that wasn't going to be easy.

Chapter Fourteen

Heart to Heart

HALFWAY BACK TO THE CABIN AND TRUDGING dejectedly along the ridge path, Noah happened to look down towards the cove and there was Millicent, sitting in the sand a short distance from the water's edge, gazing out towards the horizon. Noah paused for a moment, pondering the best way to start telling her what he needed to say, but no definite opening line came to him, so with a sigh of resignation, he turned left and began to make his way carefully down the steep rocky slope towards her, telling himself he'd just have to play it by ear.

When he reached the sand, he kicked off his shoes and

socks and left them where they fell. He walked closer and finally dropped into a sitting position a few feet to her right.

There was a long silence as they both sat there, staring out at the horizon. Then: "I thought you were supposed to be writing," he said.

She didn't turn her head to look at him. "Couldn't seem to get the ball rolling," she said. "I thought a short visit here might get the old creative juices flowing. But . . . nothing's coming." She sighed. "The Captain would have loved it here," she said.

Noah nodded. "I expect so," he said.

"I miss him so much. You expect, of course, that you'll miss somebody when they're gone, but nobody ever really explains how completely you will miss them; how every single day will seem meaningless without them in it. How even the simple things . . . making a cup of tea . . . going for a swim . . . reading the newspaper . . . will all seem so pointless." She reached out a hand and doodled a pattern into the sand with an index finger. "Where did you get to?" she asked.

"I went to see Mr Finlay," said Noah. "I wanted to ask if he would let me use his short wave radio."

"I see. And did he?"

Noah shook his head. "It's broken," he said.

"Oh dear. Well, that'll be jolly handy if ever we really do need to contact the outside world." Millicent studied him with interest. "So, what's his place like? Worth a visit?"

"Not really. Bit of a dump, to be honest. He's trying to hatch out some eggs . . ."

Millicent smothered a laugh and he could imagine what she was thinking.

"Not like that," he said. "I mean, he's not sitting on them or anything. But he has the heating cranked up until the place is sweltering." He glanced at her slyly. "He knew all about our ghost, though."

"Did he really?" Millicent looked irritated now. "Noah, you didn't go blabbing to him about seeing something last night, did you? What will he think?"

"I don't care what he thinks!" he assured her. "And I didn't have to blab about anything. He told me that everybody that's ever stayed in that cabin has seen the same thing. An old man with white hair."

Millicent grimaced. "Yes, I've no doubt he said something like that. It's probably what they tell all the tourists."

Noah did a double take. "Wh . . . what tourists? There aren't any!"

"No, but perhaps they're looking to develop the idea. You know how they are in these parts. Plant the seeds, let the idea catch on . . . next thing you know they'll be running boat trips out here. "Visit the haunted island for half a crown!" The Scottish love their ghost stories. You only have to listen to Mr Morrison."

Noah actually laughed at that. "Mr Finlay wouldn't be interested in that sort of thing. He's an orni . . . an orni . . ." He struggled to remember the word. "A bird-lover. He just wants to protect the birds on the island and make sure that nobody steals their eggs. The last thing he wants is hordes of tourists tramping around. But there have been other people that have stayed in the cabin . . ."

"Oh, have there really?"

"Yes, and none of them have managed more than one night in the place." Noah made a dismissive gesture. "Mr Finlay also said . . ."

"Go on."

Noah took a deep breath. "He said we should get out of the cabin tonight, before it gets dark. He said it was dangerous to stay there." Noah wasn't exactly sure why he was attributing Coira's words to Mr Finlay – he just knew that if he first had to explain to Millicent that he'd been talking to a girl who'd died over 400 years ago, there was no chance on earth that she would take him seriously. This way, he figured, she might at least give his words some consideration.

"Noah," she said. "If that's intended as a joke . . ."

"It's not," he assured her. "Mr Finlay told me that Mr Crannach died angry and he was a . . . what did he call it? A restless spirit . . . and that he's most powerful when it's . . ."

Millicent made a sound then, a kind of exasperated groan.

"What kind of an irresponsible idiot *is* this man!" she cried. "First he tells you that the poor wretch committed suicide, which is bad enough and now he claims he's a ghost! Who in their right mind would say any of that to an impressionable child?"

"I'm not a child," interrupted Noah. "I'm ..."

"I've a jolly good mind to go around to that shack of his and give him a piece of my mind. Where exactly is it? I might just go there right now."

"No, don't do that." She was starting to get to her feet so he reached out and grabbed her arm, pulled her down again, perhaps a little more roughly than he'd intended. "He ... he's just being a good neighbour, that's all. He's worried about us. You see, Mr Crannach found out about his ancestor, Obediah Crannach, the man who ran the old leper hospital on the cliff top. He found out that he'd been stealing from his patients and ..."

"Where does all this nonsense come from?" cried Millicent. "I swear this Mr Finlay seems to have missed his vocation! He should be in the same business as me. Making things up for a living."

"He's not making anything up. It's all in Obediah Crannach's journal. Here, you can read it for yourself..." Noah put a hand in his pocket, looking for the exercise book, but there was nothing there. He stifled a curse. "I must have left it in the hospital," he said. "But it'll still be there. I can get it for you, if you like."

"The hospital?" Millicent looked at him in exasperation.

"What were you doing up there?"

"I went and had a look around it. It's a horrible place, but . . . well, I think we should be able to sleep there tonight. The roof's mostly sound and . . ."

"What are you babbling about?" She glared at him. "Why would I want to go and sleep in the hospital? We have a perfectly good place to sleep already."

"But Mr Finlay says . . ."

"Frankly, I don't care what Mr Finlay says! Who is he anyway? Probably some raving lunatic! Clearly spent far too much time out here alone. I shouldn't have even let you go over there by yourself."

"Oh, is that right? You'd happily let the Adventurers visit him though, wouldn't you?"

Now she looked baffled. "What on earth are you on about?" she cried.

"Well, in your books, they are always running off to talk to strange people, aren't they? They leave their homes for weeks on end and nobody so much as raises an eyebrow . . . they go creeping about in the dark chasing thieves and spies and villains of all shapes and sizes. And I'll tell you something else. If Douglas came to you and said you shouldn't stay in that cabin, you wouldn't question him, would you?"

"That's just ridiculous," she told him. "Douglas is a fictional character!"

"Yes, but you're always talking about him as if he's real – as though you wish he was . . . and if he did somehow come to life, then you'd sing a different tune about all this, wouldn't you? And if I was more like him . . . then perhaps you'd listen to *me* for once."

"I haven't the faintest idea what you're talking about," Millicent assured him. She lifted a hand to her brow. "You're actually giving me a headache!" she complained. She got to her feet. "Well, anyway, you've managed to spoil this for me, so I may as well head back and . . ."

"Pretend to write," he snapped, with a malice that surprised him.

The barb hit home. He saw her eyes fill with tears and was surprised how pleased he was to witness it.

"I don't know why you have to be so perfectly beastly to me," she gasped. "All I've ever done is give you everything you ever wanted. You never went short of a single thing. So why you would say something like that is quite beyond me. Don't you think I know I'm failing at the one thing I used to be so good at?"

He felt suddenly ashamed of himself. "Oh, look I'm . . . sorry," he said. "I didn't mean that. I was angry, that's all. "He got to his feet and went to her, took her hands in his. "Listen . . . I just want to make you understand how worried I am about what could happen if we stay in that place any longer. I wouldn't want anything bad to happen to you."

"Hmmph!" Millicent shook her head. "I think I'm beginning to understand where all this is coming from," she said.

He looked at her doubtfully. "Really?" he murmured.

"Absolutely. When Mr Morrison returns on Saturday, I believe we'll go back to the mainland with him . . ."

"That's great news!" Noah felt like raising a fist in the air. "But . . . that's five days away! What if . . .?"

"And when we are back, perhaps we'll arrange for you to *see* somebody . . ."

He let go of her hands. "What do you mean?" he murmured.

"Perhaps I . . . haven't fully realised how much the loss of your father has affected you," said Millicent.

"Oh, no, it's not that. It . . ."

"We never really got the chance to talk, did we? What with you being away at school so much and me locked up in the study with my work. There must be people who know all about these things, Noah. People you could unburden yourself to. You know, they say that talking something through with a trained professional is as good as any kind of medicine you might be prescribed, so . . ."

"You think I'm . . ." He couldn't seem to find the right words. "You're saying I need help?"

"Noah, I'm only thinking about what would be best for you. I believe that you've allowed things to fester in your mind for far too long. That's what all this nonsense is about, isn't it? It's your attempt to make sense of the world. I understand, I really do. It can be a confusing place. But we'll sort everything out once we're home. I'm sure if you just talk to the right people, all these worries you have will seem insignificant." She smiled at him. "Anyway, I'll leave you here to think things over for a bit. And I'll get some lunch ready. You didn't even eat breakfast earlier, did you? You must be starving."

She turned and walked away across the beach, heading towards the rocky incline. "Head back whenever you're ready," she shouted, without even looking over her shoulder.

Noah turned away and dropped back onto the sand, burying his face in the palms of his hands. Well, that had gone perfectly, he told himself. He had failed to convince Millicent of anything except the possibility that he needed psychiatric help. Perfect. And worst of all he still had to face up to the prospect of another night in the cabin.

It wasn't something he was looking forward to.

Chapter Fifteen

Night Must Fall

NOAH LAY FULLY DRESSED ON HIS BED, ONE HAND gripping his torch, ready to flick it on if he should need it. He was determined not to fall asleep, but a couple of hours had passed since he and Millicent had gone to their respective rooms and he was horribly aware of a powerful weariness descending on him.

He had decided against hanging a blanket over the window tonight, thinking that it might be just the thing to lure Mr Crannach back to his room in order to take it down again – but that left a rectangle of midnight blue hanging right in front of him and he somehow couldn't stop himself from gazing into those inky depths, where foliage stirred and trembled in the night winds and where he half-expected to see Coira's cloaked figure staring accusingly in at him, wondering why he hadn't taken her advice. Of course, he told himself, there was nothing to stop him from carrying his blankets outside so he could bed down in the open air – but that would leave Millicent alone and defenceless in the cabin, and somehow he couldn't bring himself to abandon her. If something bad happened, she'd need his help . . .

The leaden hours passed slowly by and still Noah clung grimly on to consciousness, but it was a struggle he was rapidly losing, his eyelids growing heavy, a dark fuzzy warmth spreading across the back of his skull . . .

He turned his head to the side at the sound of a soft click. He could quite clearly see the closed door of his room in the moonlight and as he watched in terrified silence, the handle began to turn . . .

Alarmed, he snatched in a breath, scrambled around onto his knees and lifted the torch ready to use, remembering that first time he had encountered Coira in the cave, the way she had shrunk from the battery-powered light as though it was burning her. Perhaps, Noah told himself, Mr Crannach would have a similar reaction to the torch beam . . . though, now he thought about it, the last time he had seen the old man, he'd somehow managed to walk straight through a solid wooden door. So why was he bothering to open it now?

The door creaked fully open and Noah instinctively clicked the torch switch. White light bathed the figure standing in the doorway – but he looked more indignant than pained, Noah thought – and besides, it wasn't Mr Crannach. The newcomer was tall and slim, around the same age as Noah, his short blonde hair immaculately brushed, his pale blue eyes glaring defiantly back into the light. He was dressed exactly as Noah would have expected – grey flannel shorts and a spotless white shirt over which he wore a Fair Isle tank top. He had a canvas rucksack over one shoulder and his feet were encased in sensible walking boots, as though he'd travelled some distance to be here.

"Switch that ruddy thing off," he hissed irritably and Noah could do nothing but comply.

"What are *you* doing here?" he asked.

"I've jolly well come to give you a piece of my mind," said Douglas. He walked to the foot of the bed and sat down on it. "What's all this I hear about you asking if you might be allowed to leave the island?"

"Don't start," Noah advised him. "You don't understand. I haven't the faintest idea what's going on here."

"Exactly my point! It's surely up to you to find out . . . to uncover the mystery of Inchtinn."

Noah sighed, shook his head. "This is not one of Millicent's books," he insisted. "There is *something* going on here, but it's not anything you'd understand."

Douglas scoffed. "You'll be telling me next that ghosts exist," he sneered.

"Well, why not?"

"Because they don't, you chump! It'll just be some kind of cover-up that the bad lads have invented. I've been thinking it over on the way here. My money would be on this Finlay chap. He's the one who stands to gain from frightening people off this precious island."

"Really?" Noah was baffled. "How do you figure that?"

"Simple. He's probably running some kind of a con with those eggs he goes on about all the time. He's doubtless selling them as a delicacy to people who live on the mainland, and using Mr Morrison as a go-between."

Noah gave a snort of indignation. "Don't be daft! Mr Finlay is an orni ... an orni ... a bird lover. He would never do anything like that. He's here to protect the birds, not steal their eggs."

"Well, that's what we're supposed to think, anyway," sneered Douglas. "But he doesn't fool me for a minute. And didn't Mr Morrison spend ages telling you how much he loved those eggs when he was a little boy?"

"He did, yes, but ..."

"And as for those ghosts ..." said another voice. A second figure had appeared in the doorway – a short, plump girl dressed in a red duffle coat and a matching woolly hat. She blinked owlishly at Noah through a set of horn-rimmed glasses as she approached the bed and perched herself beside Douglas. "It'll just be some of the villagers, in cahoots with Mr Finlay, and dressing up as spectres to scare off any tourists."

"What villagers?" cried Noah. "There *is* no village! And as for tourists . . . me and Millicent and Mr Finlay are the only people on the island . . ."

"So far as you *know*," Sally corrected him. "Who's to say there might not be others lurking around the place, doing Mr Finlay's bidding? Some cronies. There are always cronies! That cave you're so fond of visiting would be a perfect hideaway, don't you think? Why do you suppose that girl was so keen for you to switch off the light the first time you went in there? So you wouldn't see the rest of her gang, hiding in the shadows."

Noah shook his head. "That's just ridiculous," he said. He glanced warily towards the open doorway. "Please don't tell me that Harriet is coming here as well," he muttered.

Douglas shook his head. "We left her guarding the den," he announced. "She may be young but she's jolly *fierce*. Not like certain people I could mention." He gave Noah a scornful look. "Now look here," he continued, "what are you going to do about all this? I hope you realise you're letting the side down rather badly."

"What side? There are no sides! Look, I know you're used to

everything being done for a certain reason, but that's not what's happening here. There *is* a mystery, yes, but it goes back for centuries and there really are ghosts."

Sally giggled. "Well, they've got you convinced, obviously. But Douglas and I have seen enough of these things to know that there's always a perfectly reasonable explanation for them."

"It'll be the eggs," said Douglas, confidently. "You mark my words."

"Have you actually *seen* the eggs?" reasoned Noah. "They're tiny. How many would you have to harvest in order to make any money on them? That's if the guillemots don't peck your eyes out first."

Sally made a face. "Don't be so beastly," she said. "Mr Finlay only told you that to keep you away from his precious eggs."

Noah looked from Sally to Douglas and back again. Both of them had supercilious smiles on their clean-scrubbed faces, the kind of smiles that announced to the world that they were always right and that there could be no other explanation for what was happening on Inchtinn, than the one that they had cooked up together. In that moment, Noah knew exactly why he hated them so much. Perhaps, he thought, he had always hated them, even when he was too young to realise it.

"Get out," he said quietly.

Douglas and Sally looked at each other, as though neither of them could quite believe what they'd just heard.

"I say," muttered Douglas. "There's no need for that."

"We're only trying to help," insisted Sally.

"I don't need your help," Noah told her. "Please, just go and let me sort this out for myself."

Douglas scoffed. "How do you expect to do that?" he sneered. "A boy who's afraid of the water!"

Sally giggled. "Noah, who's afraid of the water!"

"Shut up!" protested Noah. "You'll wake Millicent."

But the two of them were chanting now, grinning as they did so. "Noah's afraid of the water, Noah's afraid of the water, NOAH'S AFRAID OF THE . . ."

A sudden scream seemed to echo throughout the cabin.

Noah jolted abruptly awake to find that he was still stretched out on the bed with the torch clutched in one hand. Of Douglas and Sally, however, there was no sign. He looked frantically around.

"What . . . who . . .?" He sat up on the bed, looking this way and that, trying to make sense of what was happening; and then the scream came again, a wild cry of absolute terror. Noah had never heard Millicent cry out in such a way before, but there was no mistaking her voice. His heart thudding in his chest, he scrambled off the bed and threw open the door, switching on the torch as he did so and directing a powerful beam of light into the main room. At that same moment, the door to Millicent's bedroom crashed open and she came running out, dressed in her nightgown and yelling like something demented. She caught sight of Noah and ran to him, sobbing.

"He's in my room!" she yelled, pointing back towards the open door. "I woke up and he was standing over me. Noah, his face . . ."

She broke off as somebody came out of her room, the same haggard, white-haired man that Noah had seen the previous night. His face was arranged into an expression of pure rage and his hands were extended in front of him, fingers extended like claws. He opened his mouth and emitted an ear-shattering bellow. Noah actually felt the wind of the old man's cry gusting into his face, carrying a smell of corruption.

"We have to get out," shouted Noah, over the tumult, and he started towards the door, just as one of the cardboard boxes of provisions on the floor exploded upwards, scattering its contents in all directions.

Millicent cried out and covered her face with her hands and Noah had a moment to realise that he had never seen her like this before – his indomitable mother for once, was scared almost witless. If the situation hadn't been so terrifying, he might actually have savoured this moment, but then the big sheath of typing paper on the pine table was picked up and scattered into the air as though hit by an invisible force. That actually registered with Millicent, kindling a little flourish of defiance in her. "My writing!" she cried and made a move towards the table, clearly with the intention of rescuing the few pages she had actually managed to compose earlier.

"Leave it!" cried Noah. He tried to pull her back but she broke free of him and ran towards the table – at which point, her typewriter suddenly lurched upwards, span around in the air and then hurtled straight at her.

Noah saw what was about to happen and opened his mouth to yell a warning, but it was too late. The typewriter flew a vicious arc and connected with Millicent's forehead with a hideous thud. She went down like a felled tree, her shoulder blades smashing against the bare wooden boards, raising clouds of fine dust. Her bare legs shuddered, her heels drumming spasmodically on the floor and then were still.

"Mother!" The word that Noah never used spilled unbidden from his lips and he ran to her. Then he was kneeling beside her, cradling her in his arms, looking in the light of the torch at the ugly gash on her white forehead, pumping a torrent of dark blood. He shook her, desperately, but she was completely unresponsive, her eyes closed, her mouth hanging open. Then Noah remembered Mr Crannach.

He turned his head to look. The old man was still framed in the bedroom doorway, his dead eyes glittering with feral malevolence. He was moving closer to Noah, seemingly intent on harming him too. He made a gesture with one hand and

Millicent's precious gramophone lifted into the air, whizzed past Noah's head and smashed to pieces against the wall behind him. Noah nearly broke and ran at that moment, but knew that Millicent was too heavy for him to carry and that he could not – *would* not leave her. So he directed the torch full into the old man's face, hoping against hope that he would shrink from the light. He did not. He flung back his head and let out a roar so powerful, it seemed to shake the entire cabin. Noah felt an incredible power sweep into him, picking him up and flinging him across the room as though he weighed nothing. He struck the wall and slid down with a groan, the breath driven out of him.

Mr Crannach took another threatening step closer . . .

And then something materialised in the air between Mr Crannach and Noah, a slight, transparent figure in a shapeless robe, her back turned to him.

"Wait!" screamed Coira, and the old man froze in his tracks, mouth open. "Please," she whispered. "Please don't hurt them. They don't mean you any harm."

Mr Crannach hesitated. The blazing eyes seemed to calm a little.

Noah seized the chance to speak. "I . . . I know what happened to you," he gasped. "I know about the hospital . . . about what happened there."

Mr Crannach stood and gazed at Noah, watching him

intently. "I . . . I know about Obediah," continued Noah, telling himself that as long as he kept talking, he and Millicent might still have a chance. He waved a hand at the transparent shape still hovering between him and Mr Cranach. "Coira told me everything. I know you talked to her too. She told me what it was like at the hospital. How the . . . how the patients were cheated by your ancestor . . . and how when you found out about it, you . . . you couldn't live with the knowledge. And . . . I understand you're angry but . . . you cannot let yourself become evil because of it. That would make you . . . every bit as bad as he was."

There was a long silence then. Mr Crannach's head seemed to nod very slightly, but he made no attempt to move, just stood there, staring silently at the two people on the floor of his cabin. Then, he lifted one arm and pointed a long index finger towards the door.

He spoke one word in an eerie hiss. "Leave," he said.

Noah licked his lips. "I can't leave," he murmured. "Not . . . not yet. My mother is hurt . . ." He scrambled back to her and tried shaking her again, but there was no reaction. He looked back at Mr Crannach. "Please," he whispered. "You have to give us more time."

The old man's features arranged themselves into a grimace and a low growl escaped from him. He took another step forward.

"Please," whimpered Noah. "You have to excuse us. We didn't know about you . . . or what happened here. Just give me till daybreak. Then we'll be gone. I promise."

Another silence. The old man's expression calmed. As Noah watched, his figure gradually began to fade – and then, quite suddenly, he was gone. Coira's figure remained for a few moments longer and then it too became more transparent and vanished. Noah returned his attention to Millicent. Her face was now a fright mask beneath rivulets of blood. Noah remembered that somewhere in that jumble of scattered boxes there had been a first-aid kit. He laid Millicent's head gently on to the floor, got up and used the torch to hunt through the debris, until he found what he was looking for, a small white bag with a prominent red cross on it. He carried it back to Millicent, hunted through the contents and found a bottle of antiseptic and some cotton wool. He poured spirit over the deep cut on her head, half-expecting the sting of it to revive her, but still there was no reaction. He swabbed her face clean, and located a cotton dressing and a strip of Elastoplast, which he stuck in position across the wound. Looking through the contents by torchlight, he found a small bottle of smelling salts and felt his hope rise. He knew what that stuff could do. He uncapped it and held it under Millicent's nose, thinking that one sniff of the pungent contents would make her suddenly come awake again – but still, there was no reaction, and he felt his anxiety deepen. He was pretty sure that she was still breathing, but he wasn't certain how to check for vital signs and found himself wishing that Douglas really were here. He'd know exactly what to do.

He sat holding Millicent close to him and the hours stretched slowly by until finally a glow of light began to appear in the window. By then, Noah had his plan pretty much figured out. If Millicent still hadn't woken, he'd run to Mr Finlay's shed and ask him for help. All right, so the radio wasn't working but the ornithologist would surely have a better idea about first aid than a fourteen-year-old boy. At any rate, Noah couldn't think of a better plan.

When it was finally light enough to see without the torch, he ran to Millicent's room and pulled the covers and a pillow from her bed. He returned, slid the pillow under her head and then draped the blankets across her sprawled figure, tucking her in. As a final measure, he ran to the pump in the yard and filled a tin mug with drinking water, which he set down beside her, just in case she woke up while he was gone. He kneeled beside her and studied her face, aware now that blood was already soaking through the dressing on her forehead. He considered replacing it before he left, but decided that he couldn't afford to waste any more time.

"I'm going to get help," he told her – and he reached out and squeezed one of her hands. It felt horribly cold in his grasp so he tucked it under the covers, then got up and walked to the door. He hesitated for a moment and looked back.

"Don't give up," he told her. Then he opened the door, stepped outside and pulled it shut behind him.

He took a deep breath and began to run as fast as his legs could carry him.

Chapter Sixteen

The Birds

HE POWERED HIS WAY UP THE STEEP SLOPE, where it passed through the narrow opening in the basalt rocks, feeling the pull of the climb in his back and calves, but staying with it anyway, because he knew that every second mattered. The sooner he could get Mr Finlay to his mother, the better.

Almost before he knew it, he was passing through the flanking ranks of nesting birds, dotted amongst the jagged rocks, but something was different today. Perhaps his natural agitation had somehow passed itself on to them. As he ran by, they started shrieking indignantly, fluttering their wings and powering themselves up into the air. One bird soared past his head, missing him by a matter of inches and he winced, but dared not slow his pace. He put his head down and kept on going, so he didn't notice the next bird, a sleek black and white creature, like a magpie with an elongated neck, until it flashed right past him and he felt a sudden stinging sensation in his right cheek.

He stumbled to a halt and raised a hand to touch the place that hurt. His fingers came away streaked with blood. "Oh no," he whispered. "Not now."

He shook his head, stumbled on his way again and another bird flashed past his vision, a moving blur of monochrome, so he lifted his jacket over his head and kept going, keeping his gaze on the twisting track beneath him, not wanting to put a foot wrong and fall onto those jagged rocks. That was when he nearly tripped over something and, despite all of his urgency, he slowed to a halt and looked back at what it was. A khaki rucksack was lying on the ground, as though it had been dropped there. He didn't need to look twice to recognise it as the one that belonged to Mr Finlay. But why would he leave his bag lying here? Was he around somewhere, scrambling about in the rocks, looking for nests?

Then, Noah noticed something even more puzzling, a few steps further on. A tiny fluffy black chick lay on the ground, a short distance from the bag. Its neck was stretched out, its beak open and it appeared to be dead. One of the hatchlings, Noah wondered? He recalled what Mr Finlay had told him. The early hours of the morning were the best time to introduce a chick to prospective new parents. Had Mr Finlay been out trying to do exactly that? Was he somewhere close by?

Noah lifted his hands to either side of his mouth and let out a shout. "Mr Finlay!" he yelled. "Are you there?"

It was entirely the wrong thing to do. His words echoed around the cliffs and the birds reacted instinctively to it. Suddenly, the air was filled with moving shapes, soaring and wheeling around him, most of them those distinctive black and white birds, making angry shrieking noises. One of them came zooming straight for his head and he was forced to swing an arm at it, deflecting it away in a frantic scuffle of feathers.

Now it occurred to Noah, that this part of the track skirted a steep drop to his right-hand side. He imagined Mr Finlay, trying to reach a particular nest, perhaps one located in the cliff face that descended so perilously to the side of the track. And he pictured Mr Finlay, still muggy from the whisky he had drunk the previous night. What if one of the guillemots had flown straight at his face, as he was standing with his back to the cliff? Noah realised that the black and white birds must be the very ones that Mr Finlay had warned him about. What if one of them had attacked him as he was preparing to climb down? But no, he told himself, Mr Finlay was an experienced man, he'd be prepared for something like that . . . wouldn't he?

A terrible conviction overcame him. Instinctively, he dropped onto his hands and knees and edged carefully closer to the drop. He craned his head slightly forward to look over the edge.

A gasp spilled from him and his eyes filled involuntarily with tears. He couldn't stop himself. Mr Finlay was lying some twenty feet below, his back arched across a craggy outcrop to an impossible degree. For a moment, Noah thought that the man was wearing a pair of black sunglasses, but then he remembered what the ornithologist had told him – how the birds sometimes went for the eyes. They had clearly been working on him as he lay there dying.

Nausea rose in Noah's throat and he twisted around into a sitting position with a slow groan. Just for a moment, he considered making the perilous climb down the cliff to the fallen man, to see if he could be helped in any way, but he quickly discounted the idea. There was no chance he could still be alive. No, that would be a waste of precious time, time that Noah and Millicent simply didn't have. He would have to make his way back to the cabin and think of something else. Who knew? He might get there, only to find that Millicent was awake . . .

He got back to his feet and turned around. A blur of black and white sped through the air and rushed straight at

his face. Something sharp caught him a stinging blow just above his right eye. He yelled, raised his hands and without thinking, took an involuntary step backwards. His foot found only empty air and he felt himself overbalancing. A thrill of terror pulsed through him as he fell, but he resisted the natural impulse to twist around. He dropped past a blur of grey rock, flung out his hands and one of them connected with a flat edge of hard, smooth stone, abruptly stopping his downward momentum. He jerked to a halt with a wrench that nearly tore his arm from its socket and cried out with the pain of it, but somehow, he made his other hand scrabble about on the basalt to find purchase. By some miracle, he managed it. He hung there for a moment, trying to recover his erratic breathing, telling himself that everything would be all right, he just needed to calm himself. When he finally summoned the courage to look up, he saw that he had dropped perhaps ten or twelve feet. But, he felt a surge of hope as he told himself that, if he was careful, he should be able to climb back up to the track . . .

A sudden squawk a short distance to his left made him turn his head in dismay. He saw that there was a shallow ledge, a few feet from his head and on that ledge, in a slight depression, there was a nest. On the nest sat a guillemot, gazing at him with round, black button eyes. Noah could just see part of a speckled greenish-white egg beneath its rump. The bird was raising the feathers around its neck, its open beak revealing a bright vermillion throat.

Noah somehow managed not to yell out loud. He started looking frantically around for a foothold so he might push himself a step higher, but then a shriek in the air behind him made him turn his head in that direction. Another bird was on him in an instant, a vengeful chattering thing intent on his destruction. Its sharp beak hammered at his throat, stinging like a darning needle, while the female on the nest cheered on her partner's efforts. Noah risked removing one arm to flail at the guillemot and it flapped away, complaining loudly. Noah swung back around, resumed his hold and started lifting his right leg, prodding the rock with his toe in a desperate attempt to find purchase. More by accident than design, his foot slotted into a recess and he pushed himself a step higher, reaching up with his left hand until he had a place for that too. *Now for the left leg*, he thought grimly.

And the guillemot was back, intent on revenge and Noah knew only too well what such a bird was capable of, having just witnessed Mr Finlay's crumpled body on the rocks far below. This time, the target was the top of Noah's left ear and he felt it gripped by an unbelievable force and ripped open. He bellowed in agony, swung his arm away from the rocks and somehow managed to connect with the bird's breast, swatting it aside in a frenzied flapping of black and white.

"Stay away from me!" he screamed and weirdly, in that moment, he did not picture the bird, but the astonished face of Mr Greer, his PT instructor from school. He didn't pause to consider why he had seen that particular image. He found his next foothold and then his next handhold and he moved quickly up the rock face, powered more by frantic terror than by anything else, because he knew that one more attack could send him plunging back down the cliff to join Mr Finlay. Finally, he was able to clutch a handful of tenacious roots bordering the edge of the track and haul himself up the remaining distance.

He collapsed onto solid ground with a gasp of relief and reached up to touch his lacerated ear, coating his fingers with blood. It hurt like anything, but he didn't have time now to dwell on his injuries. He got around onto his knees and looked helplessly down at the still figure of Mr Finlay, who seemed to be studying him intently with those empty eye sockets.

"I'm sorry I couldn't help you," whispered Noah.

He thought about saying a prayer or something, but decided he dare not waste any more time. The sky was still full of furious birds, and they wouldn't calm down until they had the entire area to themselves. No, he would have to head back to the cabin and check on Millicent, he decided.

Then he'd see what was to be done.

Raising his jacket up over his head, he started back the way he had come.

Chapter Seventeen

Decision Time

A T FIRST, HE FEARED THAT SHE WAS DEAD. SHE hadn't moved so much as an inch from the way he'd left her, sprawled out on the floor under her blankets, her eyes closed, her mouth still open. He remembered something that Douglas had done in one of the Adventurers books, and went to Millicent's room to poke around in her bag until he found a small powder compact she used, one that had a mirror in the lid. He returned to the main room and held it a short distance from her lips. Sure enough, the glass clouded. He allowed himself a sigh of relief. So she *was* still breathing, at least.

He took a little time to replace the dressing on her forehead, noting as he did so that a shocking black bruise was spreading outwards from the cut. As he worked with the bandages, Noah went through all the possibilities he could think of and, as he had pretty much known he would, kept coming back to the same thought – the only option that he felt was left to him. The problem was it was an idea that terrified him, filled him with a dark, overwhelming dread. But, he asked himself, what else could he do? Millicent needed help and the longer he left her lying here, the worse it would surely be for her. It was still early morning and darkness wouldn't fall until around ten o clock tonight. If his plan worked, he could have somebody back here before nightfall.

If on the other hand, it didn't work . . .

He shook his head. He couldn't allow himself to think about that. If he did, he would never be able to make himself do what he needed to. He leaned over Millicent, reached under the cover and took one of her hands in his. He was slightly cheered by the fact that it felt just a little warmer than it had before. He looked intently at her sleeping face. "Millicent," he murmured. "I know you can't hear me, but . . . I need to tell you something. I've made a decision. I'm going to try and go for help. If this doesn't work out . . ." He took a deep breath, calmed his rising terror. "If it doesn't work, at least I'll have tried."

He waited as though expecting an answer, but no sound came from her.

He got up and went to his room and removed his clothes. He found his swimming trunks and put them on. Then he donned his clothes over them, thinking that he would need to conserve as much heat as he could until the last moment. He walked back into the room and gave Millicent one last hopeful look, picturing her with her eyes open . . . but no, she still slept and it seemed to him that the bruise had grown darker in the few moments he'd been away. It was hard not to see this as some kind of premonition – as though this was a sign of death gradually exerting its hold on her.

"Please try and hold on," he said.

He went towards the door and was about to step outside, but he remembered the birds, so he grabbed an old umbrella that Millicent had left by the entrance and, suitably armed, stepped outside and closed the door behind him. He stood for a moment, feeling his spirit quail at the thought of what he was about to do, but he shook his head and started walking.

As he climbed the narrow opening between the basalt rocks, he made a point of walking slowly and making as little noise as possible, holding the furled umbrella ready to lash out if one of the birds came at him. He was aware of scores of beady black eyes watching his progress, but for now at least, the birds stayed on their nests, studying him arrogantly but making no attempt to leave the ground – and soon enough, he had passed through their watching ranks and reached the top of the ridge.

He gazed down at the cove far below him and checked that the thing he needed was still where it had been before. It was. But he wasn't quite ready to leave yet. First there was something he needed to do. He dropped the umbrella, turned to his left and climbed the last steep incline up to the cave.

He paused for a moment by the opening and slid a hand into his pocket to take out the conch, thinking that he might need to summon Coira, but there was no need. He heard her stirring in the shadows and walked a few steps into the cave until he was safely out of the glare of the sunlight. He waited until he could make out her cloaked figure.

"My mother . . ." he said. "She hasn't woken. I need to get help."

A nod of assent, but no comment

"We should have taken your advice," he continued. "I tried to persuade Millicent to leave, but she took no notice of me. Thank you for helping us before."

"There wasn't much I could do," said Coira.

"You helped us. If you hadn't come when you did I don't know what might have happened. But my mother . . ." He tried to control the rising tremor in his voice. "Coira, she's badly injured. I'm afraid she might die."

"What are you going to do?" Coira asked him, calmly.

"The only thing I can. I'm going to try and swim to the mainland." He could hardly believe he was saying those words.

"You never know," he added, "I . . . I might spot a boat on the way over there. I might not have to swim all the way."

"You are a strong swimmer?" she asked him.

"I wouldn't say that. I *can* swim, but . . . well, I haven't for a very long time. Because of something that happened to me. But I have to try. There's a big hunk of wood down on the cove. I thought I could use that as a float. It's what your father did."

"Yes." She didn't add, "*My father who never came back,*" but it hung in the air, unspoken.

"I just thought I should . . . say goodbye," he murmured. "In case . . . you know . . . in case I don't make it back here."

"You will come back," she assured him.

"You can't know that."

"No, but I believe you will. And . . . I will . . . try and help you."

He almost laughed at that. "How do you intend to do that?" he asked her. "You can't even come out into the sunlight."

"No . . . it's hard to explain. But I will try to help."

He nodded. He supposed he couldn't ask for anything more than that.

"Coira," he murmured.

"Yes, Noah?"

"If we'd met when you were still . . . well, alive . . . do you . . . do you think we'd have been friends?"

There was a lengthy pause as though she was considering his question carefully. "Yes," she said at last. "I'm sure we would."

"Good. Well then . . . I . . . suppose I'd better get moving."

"You will make it back," she said again. "I am sure of it."

He wished he could be as confident as she was. He turned away and walked out of the cave. As he started the long descent to the beach, he was somehow aware of her eyes on him the whole way.

It seemed to take an age to reach the sand – and once on it, he was uncomfortably aware of the words inscribed on the basalt wall away to his left. GOD HAVE MERCY ON US. He thought he knew now who had chiselled it there. Somebody from the hospital, maybe one of the *foul clengers*, sent out to burn bodies on the cliff top and taking a break from his grisly work. It must have felt to that man as though all hope was gone.

Noah walked across the expanse of white sand to the opposite wall and examined the sun-bleached pallet that he had noticed on his first visit here. It was hard not to think that it had been waiting for him all this time – as though it somehow knew it would be needed in due course. He took hold of it and pulled it free from the sand. It was cumbersome and by the time he had dragged it to the shoreline, he was sweating in the gathering sunlight, but he told himself that might be a good thing, because once he immersed himself in that chilly water, he would be far from hot. He removed his clothes and left them in a tidy pile beyond the point where the tide might reach them. He even rolled up his socks and tucked one into each shoe. For some reason he couldn't exactly explain, he took the conch shell from his jacket and tucked in into the secure pocket of his swimming trunks. He took a last look up towards the cave and fancied that he could just make out Coira's shape in the cave mouth and he was reminded of the first time he had seen her. He stood for a very long time, steeling himself, trying to gather his courage, still aware of the seconds ticking away. As he stood there, he searched his mind for another possibility, something, anything other than this . . . but he came back empty.

"Just do it!" he shouted, annoyed now at his own faint-heartedness. And he pictured what Douglas would do. He wouldn't be standing around dithering like this. He'd be out of his clothes and into that water without a moment's hesitation. He needed right now to be more like Douglas. All right then. It was now or never.

He took a firm hold of the pallet and dragged it the last few steps into the shallows.

Chapter Eighteen

Big Fish

THE SHOCK HIT HIM LIKE A SLAP. THE WATER around his ankles was so bitterly cold, he very nearly turned in his tracks and ran right back to the sand – but he steeled himself, told himself that he couldn't give up that easily. He couldn't be a quitter, not when Millicent's very life was at stake. No, he had to stick to his guns here.

He pushed the pallet ahead of him, watching it critically as he did so, wanting to assure himself that it really would float and hopefully bear his weight. It dipped alarmingly for a moment, then bobbed rapidly back to the surface. The icy water flowed up around Noah's knees, his thighs, his waist and then, up over his bare chest. For an instant, it felt as though his heart had stopped beating. He gasped for breath, then grit his teeth and pushed the pallet onwards ahead of him. He hesitated only a moment longer, relishing the feel of his bare feet on the stony seabed for a last few moments – but realising that he would have to relinquish that last touch of security.

He flung himself forward, extending his arms to take a firm grip on the wood. He allowed his legs to trail out behind him and once he'd assured himself that he wasn't going to sink, he started a kicking action. There was a frustrating moment when it seemed to him that he was simply staying absolutely still on the surface of the water, but then he managed to settle into a rhythm and sure enough, he was finally aware of some forward motion. He told himself that he would surely warm up a little with the effort of propelling himself along, but for the moment at least, there was no indication of that happening. His whole body was shaking with cold.

Peering down at the sea bed below him, he saw it rapidly dropping away and felt that his confidence was in danger of falling along with it, but he shook his head and kept going, until finally he could see the ocean floor no longer and he told himself that he was committed to this now, that he was heading out into the deep, that he really was going to attempt to make the crossing. He tried not to think about what might

have happened to Coira's father all those hundreds of years ago – Coira's father who was a strong swimmer, who had been so confident that he could make the trip. Noah lifted his head and fixed his gaze on the distant line of pale blue on the horizon that he knew was the mainland. How far had Mr Morrison said it was? A little over a mile? Surely that wasn't asking the impossible, was it?

Don't think about anything else, he warned himself. *Just concentrate on getting there.*

But it was easier to think it than to do it. As he propelled himself grimly onwards, memories clamoured at the edge of his consciousness, each of them eager to swarm into his head and overpower him. Perhaps unsurprisingly, he found himself back in the boarding school swimming baths, standing poised on that high diving board, while far below him, Mr Greer gazed up at him with a knowing smirk on his porcine face. He wouldn't be quite so sure of himself now, thought Noah, if he could see what his former pupil was attempting . . . and then it occurred to Noah that if he *did* somehow manage to do this, it might be in the local newspapers and he pictured himself cutting out the article and posting it anonymously to Mr Greer. Then he imagined the man opening the envelope and examining the cutting, his arrogant smile fading as he read the words in print . . .

Noah thought that his body was beginning to warm up a little now, though it was still like pushing his way through an ice bath. He concentrated his vision on the mainland, wondering if perhaps it was already looking a little more defined, but he told himself that might just be wishful thinking on his part. The important thing was, he was doing this, he was actually doing it and if he could just keep his nerve and make it across to the other side, then perhaps Millicent would be all right and the two of them could go back to the cottage on the mainland and never think about heading out to the island again . . . though even as he thought it, he was unconvinced by his own argument because he knew now, that he had a very good reason to return there . . .

Stop letting your mind wander, he warned himself. *Keep your eyes on the mainland and don't let anything . . .*

The thought died. Noah's eyes widened. There was something in the water up ahead of him and he felt his spirits lift, because just for a moment, he actually thought it was a boat making its way straight towards him – he even raised one hand from the pallet, intending to wave at the oncoming vessel in an attempt to draw the skipper's attention . . . but then the shape in the water came fully into focus and he lowered the arm and stared in terrified disbelief at the thing that was moving rapidly through the water towards him, something that seemed to have swum in from one of his darkest nightmares . . .

There was a great humped shape ploughing through the waves – a dark, speckled mountainous thing with a huge gaping mouth. As Noah stared at in dismay, he tried to tell himself that what he was looking at was an impossibility, that there were no sea monsters, especially in these cold Northern waters . . . and yet, the thing that was coming towards him could be described in no other way.

As it moved steadily closer, pushing the waves before it, Noah began to realise just how big it really was. It towered over him and as the open mouth came closer and closer, he realised it looked big enough to take him in and swallow him whole. In that instant, he gave up all hope and told Millicent that he was sorry, that he had tried his best to no avail. He steeled himself for the impact of those gigantic jaws closing around him, just as they always did in his dreams – but even as he did so, the beast slipped suddenly into the depths and powered itself onwards just a few feet below him. Staring down, between his outstretched arms, he saw its long spotted flanks moving deeper into the grey water and only now did he fully appreciate the size of the beast. He could make out its broad, flattish head, its outstretched pectoral fins and further back, two dorsal fins guiding it through the water. Noah was like an insignificant fleck drifting above it, a tiny insubstantial thing that might be destroyed by one casual flick of the creature's tail. He did not know exactly what it was, but it was real and it was almost close enough to touch . . .

And then the creature was gone, as suddenly as it had

arrived. Noah remembered to breathe . . . and told himself that if he made it across these waters alive, he would try to identify the creature that had just passed by . . .

He realised that he had momentarily stopped propelling himself forward and stirred his half-numbed legs back into movement. He returned his gaze to the horizon and was cheered when he saw that the mainland really was starting to look a little more solid now. He thought he could make out the beginnings of proper details – cliffs, hills and areas of vegetation. He took a moment to glance back over his shoulder and sure enough, there was Inchtinn, already looking surprisingly distant on the other horizon. But then, Noah noticed something else – the dark cloud formations that were spreading out above the island, layers of tumbling, bruise black clouds – and as he stared apprehensively at them, something flickered in their midst, a pulse of pure white electricity. A storm was approaching, he decided and it was coming fast.

He turned his head away and redoubled his efforts, churning the water into foam behind him, telling himself that he couldn't afford to be caught up in the grip of a storm, remembering that time on the skiff when he and Archie had been caught in a squall, how terrified he'd been, how convinced he was that he was going to die out on the sea. Even as the thought struck him, he felt a cold wind ruffling his wet hair and the waves around him seemed to grow more choppy, more agitated.

Oh no, he thought. *This can't happen. Not now.*

A scatter of cold rain strafed him and he was aware of the light suddenly going out of the sky as clouds moved in to obscure the sun. If felt to him as though the temperature had just dropped by several degrees. The waves, previously so calm, started to obey the commands of the gathering wind, pitching and yawing, almost threatening to tear the pallet out of his numb hands. Instinctively, he pulled it closer to him, wrapped his arms around it and hung on tight. Forked lightning sliced the darkening sky into fragments and the wind began to howl, eerily, like some lost soul mourning the passing of the sunshine. And when Noah strained his eyes to look for the mainland, he realised to his horror that he could no longer make it out.

Chapter Nineteen

The Eye of the Storm

HE WAS LIKE A CORK BOBBING HELPLESSLY ON the surface of some violent rapids, desperately clinging on to the battered old chunk of wood that was his only hope of salvation as the water raised him up onto the top of a peak, then flung him down into its depths, deluging him at every plunge and threatening to tear the pallet right out of his hands. He was literally numb with cold, his eyes and ears streaming with water and, except when another lightning bolt split the heavens, unable to see where he was or even where he was going. He was sure of only one thing. If the storm didn't blow itself out soon, he would die out here. He felt exactly as he had that time on the skiff, remembering how he'd clung on to a rail, shaking with terror, while Archie had stood at the tiller, huge, indomitable, barking orders at Noah, as though refusing to acknowledge that this was anything out of the ordinary.

"Come along boy, pull yourself together, it's nothing, we'll soon ride it out!"

But this was different. Noah was completely alone and with every rise and fall, he was horribly aware of his grip on the wood weakening. It was surely only a matter of time before it was torn from his grasp and yet, he continued to pump his legs in a desperate attempt to power himself forward, even though he no longer knew which way he was supposed to be going. A desperate sadness settled over him. He imagined Mr Morrison, leaving his waterside cottage in several days" time and making the slow crossing to Inchtinn. He pictured the old man tying his dinghy up at the dock and sauntering across the beach to the cabin. He'd knock on the door and wait a while, but then there would be no answer, so he would open it and step politely inside . . . only to find Millicent's dead body sprawled out on the floor and of Noah, no sign at all . . .

Lightning flashed again with such force that the purple-white glow of it seemed to sear itself into Noah's vision. He took the opportunity to crane his head around, trying to get an indication of where he was in relation to the mainland, but the light was all too brief and, once extinguished, the dark, gunmetal grey swamped everything again. He was fighting blind. This could only end one way, he decided.

And yet he fought with every ounce of strength he had left in him, because to give in to it would be the end of not just him, but Millicent too. He imagined what would be written about her after she was gone – the children's mystery author who had died her own mysterious death. And what had happened to her adopted son? Where had he gone? Inevitably, somebody would come up with the theory that Noah must have murdered his adoptive mother – and, unable to face up to the consequences of his own actions had run up to the cliffs and flung himself off them, just like Mr Crannach before him . . .

Another wave swamped Noah and he found himself having to hold his breath as he attempted to struggle his way back to the surface. At the last moment, the wood finally buoyed him up and he was able to snatch in a breath, but as he floundered there, waiting for the next wave to smash over him, he realised there was no longer any point in fighting the inevitable. There was only one way this was going to end. When the next wave took him and lifted him up, he didn't cling on to his pallet quite so tightly – and when he dropped into the abyss, it came as no real surprise to him that it was snatched from his hands and flung contemptuously away, like a child's toy. There was a brief glimpse of it tumbling end over end across the waves and then he fell like a stone, and when he smashed feet-first into the surface of the water, he went straight through it and began to sink. He slipped down into the depths and he didn't struggle any longer . . .

Down into silence he drifted and it was so much calmer down here, so very tranquil. He glanced around but it was dark beneath the surface, he could see absolutely nothing. He realised that he had been holding his breath and decided there was little point in doing it any longer. He was sinking deeper and deeper and a strange calm overtook him and made him decide that it was time to let that final breath out . . .

And then something moved against him, something smooth and muscular and oily. Instinctively, he flung out his arms to enfold whatever it was in a tight embrace and quite suddenly, his downward momentum was being dramatically reversed, he was rising again, coming swiftly back to the surface. He broke through and let out a gasp of breath and the unseen thing was still beside him, powering him through the water. He tried to make out what it was he was clinging onto but he couldn't, he was so cold, so overwhelmed, he was on the verge of total exhaustion. Somehow, he retained his grip on the smooth, moving shape beside him, he clung on tightly to it even as darkness claimed him and caused him to drift away into oblivion, as eerie voices called his name and he shone a powerful torch beam into the entrance of a cave, where a hooded figure waited silently for him . . .

"Show me your face," he whispered and the figure moved closer...

* * *

Consciousness came back to him with the sound of shingle stirring restlessly on a beach. He opened his eyes, gazed up at a stormy sky, then coughed out a mouthful of salty water. He sat up, confused. He was still numb with the cold. He looked around and saw that he was lying on a wide stretch of beach – not the cove, he decided, no, this was a stony beach, not the one that led up to Mr Crannach's cabin, but one that he was pretty sure he had never seen before. He managed to stagger upright and stood there, swaying woozily on his feet for a moment. He found that he was standing just a short distance from the sea, the waves pounding furiously onto the shingle in front of him, as though incensed that he had somehow escaped their clutches. He looked desperately around and saw, further up the beach, a distant light in the greyness of the storm. He turned and reeled in that direction, hardly aware of the hard stones beneath his naked feet. He staggered onwards and half-way there, he lifted his hands to either side of his mouth and let out a yell.

"Help me!" he cried, but his words were blown away on the wind. He paused, tried again, louder this time. "HELP!" There was no reply so, shivering violently, he put his head down and lurched onwards. He finally crested a rise and there was a cottage ahead of him, a low white-painted building with a thatched roof and a chimney that belched smoke. He pushed open a low wooden gate and limped along a short path. Through a small window, he could see a brightly lit kitchen inside and a fire burning in a cast iron hearth. A woman was standing at a stove, heating something in a saucepan. Noah lifted a hand and slapped wearily at the window. She didn't hear him, so he hit it again, harder this time, almost hard enough to break the glass. She looked up to the window, puzzled and then her expression turned to one of shock. She opened her mouth and shouted something, then took the saucepan off the heat and hurried out of the kitchen.

Noah managed to make it to the front door and he waited for what seemed an eternity, one arm braced against the wall to keep himself upright. Finally the door opened and a middle-aged couple stood in the entrance staring out at him in astonishment. The man was stocky and bearded, the woman plain with short black hair and a ruddy complexion. They didn't say anything, so Noah spoke first in a kind of croak. He waved a hand over his shoulder.

"Please," he gasped. "Please help. My mother . . . my mother is injured. She's on Inchtinn." He half-turned to point, but a dizziness overcame him and he felt himself falling – but the man stepped forward to catch him.

"Martha, get blankets and a hot drink," he said. "I'll go for the coastguard." He lifted Noah effortlessly into his arms and carried him into the cottage. "How the hell did you get here?" he murmured.

Noah looked up at him and smiled proudly. "I swam," he murmured – and then the blackness took him.

Chapter Twenty

The Return

NOAH STOOD ON THE OLD JETTY AND STUDIED the cabin anxiously. The two men who had ferried him over in the lifeboat had told him to wait here, that on no account must he try to follow them. They hadn't really wanted him to accompany them back to the island in the first place but Noah had insisted, loudly, that he must. In the end, they reluctantly agreed; but once moored at the jetty, they'd insisted that he remain here, telling him that they didn't know what they would find in the cabin. The two men were called Alistair and Stuart and they seemed to know what they were doing. They had taken a stretcher and a whole heap of equipment into the cabin with them, but they seemed to be taking a very long time in there . . .

Noah paced anxiously around on the jetty, aware that the clothes that the people in the cottage had loaned him, clothes that belonged to their oldest son, were way too big for him, but he was glad of them anyway. While he had waited for the man to come back with the coastguard, the woman, who was called Martha, had filled a tub in her small bathroom with hot water so Noah could immerse himself and after that, he sat by the open fire with a blanket around him, sipping a big mug of the soup that Martha had been warming on the stove when he arrived.

The storm had blown itself out by the time the coastguard's boat had got there and now the last shreds of grey were dispersing as the afternoon sun gradually burned its way through the haze. On the way in, they had moved close to the rocks where Mr Finlay had fallen, close enough for Alistair and Stewart to study his fallen body through binoculars and to ascertain that there really was no chance of him having survived the fall. By now, the body was literally covered with flapping, pecking birds and Noah had found himself unable to watch. "We'll have to come back for the body later," Alistair announced grimly. "Right now, your mother is our priority."

They had been in the cabin for what seemed like hours – and Noah was on the point of disobeying their orders and walking up the beach to join them, when he heard the sound of an outboard motor approaching. He turned towards the water and was delighted to see a familiar little dinghy puttering its way towards the jetty. Mr Morrison stood in the stern, a quizzical expression on his face, one that quickly turned to a relieved smile when he saw Noah standing there. He lifted a hand to wave and Noah waved back. Mr Morrison moved back to the rudder and eased the dinghy alongside the rescue boat. He threw a mooring rope up to Noah, who secured it to a post, then ran forward to give Mr Morrison a hug as he climbed up the ladder onto the jetty.

"Now then," said Mr Morrison, looking down at Noah in surprise. "What's going on here? I picked up an alarm call over the short wave and headed straight over as soon as the storm had cleared. Where's your mother?"

Noah stepped back and pointed up the beach to the cabin. "The coastguard men are with her now. They wouldn't let me go in there."

Mr Morrison frowned. "But what on earth has happened?" he asked. "On the radio, they said something about an accident."

"Yes." Noah nodded. "That's right. Millicent had a fall. She . . . she bashed her head against the table."

He wasn't exactly sure why he hadn't told the truth about what had happened. Perhaps he feared that Mr Morrison would think he'd gone crazy.

"And who raised the alarm?" asked Mr Morrison. "Finlay?"

"No . . ." Noah studied his feet for a moment. "No, I'm sorry, but . . . Mr Finlay is dead," he murmured.

"Dead? But how . . . ?"

"He fell from the cliffs. Did you not notice, as you came in? The birds . . . ?"

Mr Morrison's eyes widened in realisation. "I saw them eating something among the rocks. I assumed it was a dead seal. Oh my stars! Then, how . . . ?"

"I raised the alarm," said Noah. "I . . . I swam over to the mainland."

Mr Morrison actually took a step back and for a moment was in danger of falling off the jetty. He stared at Noah openmouthed. "You *swam*?" He turned and gazed out towards the stormy horizon, as though trying to remind himself exactly how far it was. "But I thought . . . I thought that you were scared of water."

"I was," said Noah. "But I'm not anymore."

He was amazed to realise that this was the truth. Whatever else happened to him from here on in, he knew that he would never again experience the overpowering terror that had been with him for so long. He had conquered that fear once and all.

Mr Morrison stood for a moment, gazing across the ocean as though trying to puzzle it out. He reached up a gnarled hand to scratch his head. "You swam," he said again, as though he couldn't quite believe it. "That's over a mile. How did you . . . ?"

"I had some help," said Noah quietly and then turned, as the door of the cabin opened and the coastguard men emerged, carrying a stretcher between them. They came down the beach, taking great care not to jostle Millicent as they walked. She was stretched out under blankets, an oxygen mask covering the lower part of her face. There was some kind of a dressing on her forehead and Noah noticed that her eyes were still tight shut. The two men clumped onto the jetty, Alistair in the lead. He spotted Mr Morrison and nodded to him.

"Hello Martin," he said. "Been listening in to our radio again, have you?"

Mr Morrison gave a sheepish smile. "I have," he admitted. He nodded towards the stretcher. "How is she?" he asked.

"She's still unconscious. She has a bad concussion, I'd say, but we'll know more when we get her to the hospital." He gave Mr Morrison a sharp look. "The boy told us you brought these people over here. Is that right?"

"Well, yes," admitted Mr Morrison. "Mrs Palmer hired me to bring them. But I'm sure if I hadn't done it, somebody else would have."

"Hmm." Alistair looked far from happy. "This place is wild, Martin, it's not a holiday destination," he said. "Did you hear about Finlay?"

Mr Morrison nodded. "The lad just told me. Look, if I can help you out in any way . . ."

"No, we'll have to come back and recover the body once we've got Mrs Palmer to the hospital. Here, you two, give us a hand to lift her down, will you?" The four of them managed to get the stretcher onto the boat and Alistair and Stewart locked it into position on a wooden bench in the wheelhouse.

"Perhaps I should gather up all their things and follow you over," suggested Mr Morrison, glancing at Noah.

Alistair fixed the old man with a meaningful look. "You know what? Maybe you should bring the lad with you," he said. "There isn't a lot of room in here and it will give the docs a chance to assess things before he gets there."

Mr Morrison nodded. "Aye, that makes sense," he agreed. He looked at Noah. "If it's all right with you," he said.

"Yes," said Noah. He understood only too well what Alistair was getting at. The hospital staff would work a lot better if they didn't have an anxious child hanging on their every move. "Yes, I'll go with Mr Morrison," he agreed. He turned to look at Alistair. "Please get her to the hospital as quickly as you can," he added.

Alistair nodded. "We'll have an ambulance waiting at the Quay," he said. "She'll reach the hospital in the shortest possible time." He looked at Mr Morrison. "You can get the boy across to the Victoria?" he asked.

"Aye. I still have my old truck."

"Good. Well, we'll see you there."

Noah and Mr Morrison watched as the two men cast off. The engine roared into life and the rescue boat moved briskly away from the jetty and headed for the mainland, gathering speed as it went. Noah watched until it was little more than a black dot in the distance.

Mr Morrison put a hand on Noah's shoulder. "Try not to worry," he said. "I'm sure she'll be fine. She's a tough lady, your mother." He looked at Noah searchingly. "How did she come to fall?" he asked.

"I . . . I suppose she tripped over something. I . . . didn't see it happen. I just . . . found her lying there." Again, he couldn't bring himself to tell the old man the truth. He would though, he told himself, when the time felt right.

Mr Morrison seemed to consider this for a moment. "Well, we'd better get you packed up," he said. "The sooner we're done, the sooner we can leave." He turned and walked towards the cottage and Noah followed him. The door had been left ajar and Mr Morrison stepped into the main room, then stood, looking around in dismay. The interior was a jumble of smashed furniture, upturned cardboard boxes and scattered paper. Millicent's gramophone lay in a splintered heap and her typewriter sat on its side in the middle of the room, a bright smear of blood on its metal frame. Mr Morrison looked down at it and then turned to stare at Noah. "An accident, you said," he murmured.

Noah nodded but somehow couldn't look Mr Morrison in the eye.

"I . . . I don't think it was a good idea, coming here," he said

"It wouldn't appear so," said Mr Morrison. He frowned. "Well, we'd . . . better get ourselves organised," he said.

The two of them worked in silence for a while, repacking the unused provisions into the boxes, flinging clothes into suitcases and stacking them together in the middle of the room. Mr Morrison looked down at the typewriter. "What about this?" he asked.

"I think we'll leave it," said Noah, quickly. "It's too badly damaged." But he made a point of collecting any typed sheets of paper he could find and stacked them neatly in one of the boxes, knowing that if Millicent did wake up, it would doubtless be the first thing she asked about. Pretty soon, they had everything ready and Mr Morrison announced that they should start carrying the belongings down to the jetty.

"There's something I have to do first," said Noah. "Can you give me ten minutes or so?"

"Of course," said Mr Morrison. "Take as long as you like. I'll make a start and you can join me when you're ready."

"Thank you."

Noah hurried out of the front door and around the cabin to the back garden. He glanced back once to ensure that he wasn't being watched and then started walking quickly towards the cliff path. He moved quietly, not wanting to alert the birds but as it turned out, most of the aggressive males were nowhere to be seen. Noah realised that they were probably still congregated around Mr Finlay's body. He put the thought aside. He really didn't want to dwell on it.

* * *

He climbed the last rise to the cave mouth and stepped into the gloom. She was waiting for him, as he knew she would be, still hanging back in the shadows, her head bowed.

"Your mother is well?" she asked.

"I wouldn't say that. She was still unconscious when they took her away. They are taking her to a hospital . . . a *proper* hospital," he added, in case she was thinking of her own experiences. "Somewhere they can take care of her."

"That's good to hear," she said.

"I'll be leaving soon," he told her. "But I . . . wanted to say goodbye. And I wanted to thank you."

"Thank me?"

"Yes. That *was* you, wasn't it? I only just put it all together. The seal. You said something before about how you tried to warn me not to stay in the cabin and I didn't understand then. But that's the way you can travel in daylight, right?"

The hooded head nodded. "I don't really understand how I do it," she said. "I cannot even remember the first time it happened. There have been other creatures over the years, ones that I could send my spirit into, but lately there is one seal in particular. We seem to have a connection. And I did promise I would help you."

He smiled. "I wouldn't have made it without you," he said. "I was done for out there. I owe you my life." He thought for a moment. "I'll come back," he said.

There was a silence. "No you won't," she said, at last. "Why would you?"

"To see you again, of course! I reckon Mr Morrison will bring me if I ask him. If . . . if that's all right with you . . ."

"I *want* you to come back," she said quickly. "I will miss you Noah."

"There's just one thing though . . ."

"Yes?" He was aware of the power of her gaze fixed upon him.

"I'll only come back on one condition."

"Speak it."

"I'll come back if you let me see your face."

Another long silence, then. "I told you before. My face is not fit to be seen."

"Let me be the judge of that," he said.

"Please. Do not make me do this."

"If you want me to come back, then that's the price," he told her.

Time passed. She stood there, still considering. Then she let out a long, deep, sigh. "Once you have seen me, you won't want to return," she told him.

"I promise," he assured her. "If you let me see your face, I'll come back."

"You would not break a promise?"

He shook his head. "Never," he said.

Finally, she took a halting step towards him. Then another. A third step brought her close enough for him to see in the half-light. He caught his breath.

He only dimly registered the face that regarded him from within the hood – what struck him most about it were those large, dark eyes, gazing at him with total trust and sincerity. He realised that they were the eyes of someone that had saved his life – and that he had already seen them somewhere before.

"Thank you," he said. "You're wrong, by the way. You're perfect." He reached a hand into his pocket and pulled out the conch shell, which, secure in the pocket of his swimming trunks, had somehow survived his ordeal in the water. "What about this?" he asked her.

She lifted an almost fingerless hand in a gesture of dismissal. "It is yours now," she told him. "Keep it in memory of me."

"I'll play it for you when I come back," he said. "I'll practice a tune." He returned the shell to his pocket. "Well," he said. "I need to go now. There's someone waiting for me. Goodbye, Coira."

"Goodbye Noah," she murmured. "God speed."

He turned away and walked out of the cave. He stood for a moment, blinking in the glare of the gathering sunlight, wondering how it must feel to have spent so much time in one lonely place, staring out at the world and waiting for somebody to arrive. He shook his head, then started walking.

Chapter Twenty-One

Homeward

NOAH SAT ON THE WOODEN BENCH IN THE REAR of the boat, gazing at the approaching mainland as the heavily laden dinghy puttered sedately across the calm ocean. He couldn't help but remember how wild and inhospitable it had been only a few hours earlier. The canvas lifejacket hung on its mooring a short distance from him, but he felt no compunction to put it on for this journey. The thought astonished him. He had changed so much in just a few short days.

"Where did you get to?" asked Mr Morrison, who was sitting alongside him. "When you went off earlier?"

"Oh, I left something up on the cliffs," said Noah. "I needed to go back for it."

"And you found it?"

"Yes, I found it." Noah slipped a hand into his jacket pocket and traced the smooth surface of the conch with his fingertips.

Mr Morrison smiled. "I'm sorry your stay on Inchtinn turned out to be such a disaster," he said. "I bet you wish your mother had never decided to go there in the first place."

Noah shrugged. "My mother has always done exactly as she wants to do," he said. "I admire her for that. In fact, I'm going to try and be a bit more like her in future. I just hope she's alright," he said.

"Like I said before, she's a tough lady. I think it will take more than a wee biff on the head to slow her down."

Noah nodded. "You're probably right," he said. "I do hope so. Mr Morrison, did you ever hear anything about the cabin being haunted?"

The old man looked puzzled. "The cabin? Where you were staying? No, never. Oh, there's plenty of folk who say the *island* is haunted . . . we spoke about that before, didn't we? But the cabin? That's a new one on me. But then, I don't set any store by such nonsense. I believe in what I can see, what I can touch, what I can hear." He gave Noah a quizzical look. "Why do you ask?"

"Well, it's just that before Mr Finlay died, he . . . he told me about Mr Crannach, the old man who lived there. About how he'd killed himself."

Mr Morrison scowled. "I did hear about that," he muttered. "And I thought it a sorry tale to pass on to a youngster so I kept my peace about it. But, aye, it happened sure enough. A long time ago, mind. And nobody seems to know what drove him to it . . ."

Noah almost told Mr Morrison that *he* knew the answer to that, but stopped himself at the last moment. It would take too much explaining, he decided. It was surely best kept for when they had more time. But for now, he needed to come up with some kind of explanation.

"I think that there's something about the cabin that . . . doesn't feel right," said Noah. "I think bad things have happened there and somehow, they've sort of . . . infected it. I really think . . . if anyone else asks you about staying there, you should try and talk them out of it."

Mr Morrison looked at him. "You really think so?"

"Yes, I do."

"Well, I'd say Alistair took a dim view of me bringing the two of you over to Inchtinn in the first place. I probably haven't heard the last of that. So I'm inclined to take your advice on the matter." Mr Morrison was gazing thoughtfully out across the ocean. "You know, I was thinking . . . it's an astounding thing you did," he murmured. "It would be quite a feat for anyone but especially for someone like yourself, so nervous of the water. I remember how you were when I picked you up. How did you ever make yourself do it?"

"I don't really know. I just told myself that I had to. Believe me, if there'd been some other way, I'd have taken it like a shot. There was this old wooden pallet I found that I used as a float and I just . . . kept going . . ." He knew he couldn't explain abou the help he'd been given, but it did make him think of something else. "Mr Morrison, have you ever heard of sea monsters in these waters?"

"Sea monsters?" The old man looked puzzled. "How do you mean?"

"I saw something out here. It was like . . . the biggest fish you've ever seen . . . I mean, gigantic! It had this great big open mouth. It swam right under me and it was the size of a house. I've never seen anything like it before."

Mr Morrison pondered for a moment "Let me see now. Was it . . . all spotted like a leopard?" he asked.

Noah looked at him. "It was!" he exclaimed.

Mr Morrison looked impressed. "There *is* a creature called a whale shark," he said. "My father told me about them when I was a wee boy. He was a merchant seaman in the Far East when he was a young man and he talked about seeing them, many times, off the coast of Japan. The biggest fishes in the ocean, he said they were. They prefer the warmer waters, you see, and that's where they usually congregate. But he also told me that one time, he saw just such a fish off the coast of Fife. I didn't believe him, back then. I thought he was just trying to scare me. But I have talked to other fishermen since who claim to have seen such creatures, once in a while. A great open mouth, you say?"

"Yes," said Noah. "Like the mouth of a cave. I . . . I really thought it was going to swallow me whole."

Mr Morrison chuckled. "You'd have been in no danger of that," he assured Noah. "My father told me that whale sharks eat the smallest things in the ocean. Can you believe that? The biggest fish eating something called plankton – tiny creatures drifting around in shoals. Inside that mouth is a kind of filter that separates the plankton from the water. Like a great big sieve!" He looked at Noah admiringly. "And you saw a whale shark!" He chuckled. "I've spent most of my life hoping for a glimpse of such a beast." He shook his head. "Well, if that doesn't beat everything."

They puttered on in silence for a while, each lost in their own thoughts.

"Mr Morrison," said Noah after a while. "If I ever asked you to take me back to Inchtinn, would you do it?"

The old man seemed understandably surprised. "I thought you said I was to stay away from the cabin?"

"Oh no, not to the cabin. But the cove."

"Why would you want to go back?" he asked. "After everything that's happened there, I'd have thought you'd want to give it a wide berth."

Noah shrugged his shoulders. "There's just something about the place," he said. "I can't really explain it. There's something there that . . . haunts me. What do you think? Would you take me back if I asked you? Just for an hour or so?"

"Well, we'd have to see," said the old man.

Noah smiled. It wasn't exactly a no, then.

There was a sudden splash in the water alongside the boat and a sleek dark grey head broke the surface. The seal was swimming next to them looking intently up at Noah and once again, there was that sense of recognition, the knowledge that he had looked into those same dark eyes only a little while back.

Mr Morrison chuckled. "I see your pal is here again," he said. "Anyone would think she doesn't want you to leave."

Noah smiled. "Why do you think I just asked you to bring me back again?" he asked. "So I can see her." He leaned over the side of the dinghy and spoke softly. "I'll be back, I promise," he murmured.

The seal held his gaze for a few moments longer, then sank beneath the surface and was gone.

Epilogue

WHEN NOAH STEPPED INTO MILLICENT'S private room, he was greeted by a familiar sound – that of a typewriter being pounded furiously. He stood there, staring in open-mouthed disbelief. Millicent was stretched out in bed, propped up against a heap of clean white pillows. On an overbed table in front of her sat a gleaming new Underwood typewriter and alongside it rested a whole pile of typewritten sheets.

"Mother, what are you playing at?" cried Noah. He found he was calling her that all the time now, without even thinking about it. "It's been less than a week, the doctor said you're to take it easy!"

She stopped typing and regarded him sheepishly. The bruising on her forehead had faded somewhat over the past few days but the sutures on the cut still stood out livid red against her pale skin. "Oh, don't make such a fuss!" she chided him. "This little beauty arrived today and I simply wanted to try her out." She patted the new typewriter fondly. "I ordered her from one of those mail order catalogues and it arrived all neatly packaged, first thing this morning. Besides, the new idea was just crying out to be committed to paper."

Noah rolled his eyes. He approached the bed, set down the tin of Quality Street chocolates he'd brought her and settled himself into an easy chair.

The new idea?" he echoed.

"Yes, you remember, we discussed it. The supernatural thing."

"Oh yes." He smiled. "That one."

"Of course, in the book, it will turn out to be the villains *pretending* to be ghosts in order to keep the Adventurers away from the old lighthouse – the place where they are sending their secret codes to the enemy agents."

Noah raised his eyebrows.

"Pretend ghosts?" he murmured.

"Yes, well, I don't think my readers are quite ready for the real thing, just yet." She looked inquisitively at Noah. "Is Martin not with you?" she asked.

This was another new phenomenon. "No more "Mr Morrison." Now, she always referred to him as Martin and he usually called her Millicent. Interesting times, thought Noah, but he wasn't making any assumptions.

"He went to the cafeteria. He said he'd bring you up a cup of tea."

"Oh, excellent! He must have read my mind. He's good like that." She studied the sheet of paper in the platen for a moment as though eager to continue.

Noah shook his head. "Alicia has already put the deadline back by a month," he reminded her. "So there's really no need to be in such a tearing hurry to bash it out."

"True," she admitted. "But I don't think you appreciate how long it's been since I've felt so . . . so *driven*." She lifted a hand and traced the shape of the sutures with the tip of an index finger. "I swear that bump on the noggin put something back into place in my head . . . something that had temporarily gone askew. But, nevertheless . . ." She moved the wheeled table to one side for a moment. "Noah, we need to talk," she said.

He looked at her in surprise. "Do we?" he asked her.

"Yes, I rather think we do. How is that home help managing, by the way?"

"Oh, she's all right. She's actually a better cook than you."

"Cheek! Well, you can tell her not to get too settled. The doctor says I can come home in a few days."

"That *is* good news," said Noah. He looked hopefully at the chocolates. "You thinking about opening those?" he wondered.

"Not yet." She fixed him with a serious expression. "Have you thought any more about this school thing?"

"I have," he said.

"And you're still set on the idea?"

He nodded. "Mr Morrison says it's an excellent place. He knows plenty of people that went there and they've all come out with good prospects."

"Hmm." Millicent didn't look quite as convinced at Noah. "You may be a fish out of water there," she reminded him. "It's a decent enough grammar, I'm told, but it's for the local boys. You'll probably be the only one with an English accent. You might get ribbed for it."

Noah shrugged. "I can handle that."

She studied him for a moment. "You know, I do believe you can," she said. "Whatever happened to you out there on the water, Noah? I believe something in you must have changed."

"I think perhaps it did," he agreed. "I think I stopped being afraid of my own shadow."

She studied her hands for a moment and he was shocked to see that her eyes had suddenly welled with tears. "You must think me the most ungrateful creature on the planet," she said. "In all this time since I woke up, I don't believe I've ever thanked you for what you did for me. You . . . you truly saved my life."

He didn't know what to say to that. "I . . . I suppose I just did what needed to be done," he told her. "I really didn't stop to think about it. And I couldn't come up with any other way to help you."

"Yes, but you of all people! A boy who was nervous . . . no, *terrified* of the water. The courage that must have taken! I can barely comprehend it. And here's me, so preoccupied with that damned book, I haven't even taken the time to tell you how proud I am of you."

He was feeling rather uncomfortable now. "Those chocolates . . ."

"Never mind the damned chocolates! This is important, Noah. Come here."

"Oh, there's really no need . . ."

"Come here, I said." He got dutifully up from the chair and moved into her embrace. She held him against her and he was aware of her sobbing silently against his cheek. It shocked him, because he didn't think he'd ever witnessed her crying before, not even the night she'd learned of Archie's death.

"I know I haven't been the best Mother," she whispered.

"Oh, you've been all right . . ."

"No, listen to me! I don't deserve you. Noah McCallum, I want you to know that you are without doubt, my absolute hero."

He pulled back a little and feigned a surprised look. "What, not Douglas?" he asked her.

She snorted. "Douglas is a fictional character," she told him. "Right here, I have the real thing. The boy who braved the ocean for his mother." She seemed to think for a moment. "You know, there might be a book in that," she mused.

"Don't you dare!" he warned her. "Now, what about those Quality Street?"

She laughed. "Open them," she said. "If you must. But make sure you leave me the purple ones."

Noah picked up the tin, returned to his seat and set about breaking the seal on the metal lid. He regarded the brightly wrapped sweets within, but paused for a moment before taking one. He looked at Millicent.

"About what happened to us," he said. "On the island. How much do you actually remember?"

"Not a great deal," she told him. "I remember waking up and seeing that frightful figure standing over my bed, looking down at me. I remember being absolutely terrified and running into the next room . . . then . . ." She held out her hands to either side. "Then fireworks followed by darkness. I'm afraid I really can't put *that* in a book." She looked towards the open door. "I wonder where Martin is with that cup of tea?" she murmured. "I'm parched." Noah noticed the way her gaze kept moving sideways to the Underwood waiting on the table.

"Oh, go on," he said. "I can see you're dying to."

"Just to the end of the chapter," she murmured. "It's really getting rather exciting. The Adventurers are trapped in a cellar and all this flood water is coming in." She slid the table back into position, studied the paper for a moment and then started typing again, her fingers flying across the keys with practised precision.

Noah smiled. He sat back in his chair, reached into the tin and took out a chocolate. As the typewriter keys chattered, he unwrapped his chosen sweet very slowly and then, with a sigh of pleasure, he slipped it into his mouth.

THE END

Acknowledgements

As ever, with the creation of a new book, there are several people to thank.

To Debbie Jane Williams, Hazel Holmes and the rest of the team at UCLan Publishing – thank you for working so tirelessly on its behalf.

Thanks are also due to Helen Crawford White for the enchanting cover design and to Miranda Harris for the charming interior illustrations.

But mostly, I would like to thank the complete stranger, who, a year or so back, was sitting opposite me on a train as I travelled to a school visit in Fife.

As we clattered across the Forth Bridge, the man tapped

his companion on the shoulder, pointed out of the window and said, 'Look! That's the old leper island.'

I didn't say anything at the time, but I certainly took notice – and those six words provided the seeds from which *Inchtinn: Island of Shadows* eventually grew.

Inchtinn isn't a real place. It's an amalgam of the many tiny islands that dot the Firth of Forth, all of which are worthy of a visit.

Though if you do choose to see them, I sincerely hope you have an easier time of it than Noah does.

Also by Danny Weston

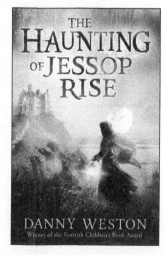

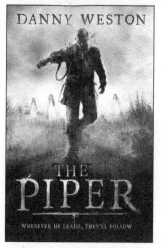

If you liked this, you'll love . . .

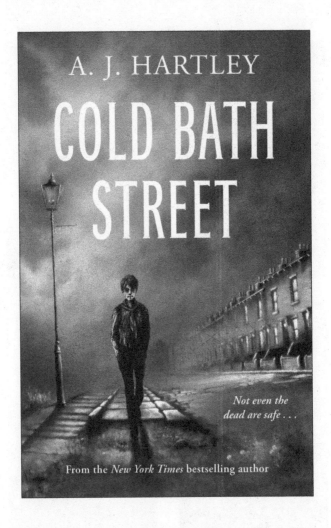

A. J. HARTLEY

COLD BATH STREET

*Not even the
dead are safe . . .*

From the *New York Times* bestselling author

www.uclanpublishing.com

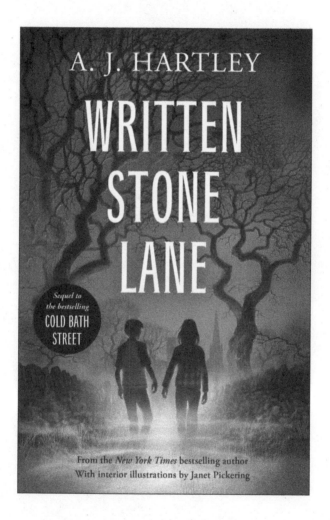

A. J. HARTLEY

WRITTEN STONE LANE

Sequel to
the bestselling
COLD BATH
STREET

From the *New York Times* bestselling author
With interior illustrations by Janet Pickering

www.uclanpublishing.com